IMPOSSIBLE

Gary H. Miller
and
Bob Tischler

Acknowledgements

Hungry Heart
by Bruce Springsteen.
Copyright @ 1980 Bruce Springsteen (ASCAP).
Reprinted by permission. International copyright secured.

All rights reserved.

My Life
Words and Music by Billy Joel
Copyright (c) 1978 IMPULSIVE MUSIC
All Rights Administered by ALMO MUSIC CORP.
All Rights Reserved Used by Permission

Reprinted by Permission of Hal Leonard Corporation

Jersey Girl
Words and Music by Tom Waits
Copyright (c) 1980 Fifth Floor Music Inc.
All Rights Administered by BMG Rights Management (US) LLC
All Rights Reserved Used by Permission

Reprinted by Permission of Hal Leonard Corporation

Copyright © 2014 by Gary H. Miller and Bob Tischler

ISBN-13: 978-0692379264 (Facetious, Inc.)
ISBN-10: 0692379266

This is a work of fiction. Any names, characters, places, and incidents either are the product of the authors' imagination or are used fictionally, and any resemblance to actual persons, living or dead, businesses, companies, events or locals is entirely coincidental.

All Rights Reserved

No part of this document may be reproduced or transmitted in any form or by any means, electronic, mechanical, photocopying, or otherwise, without written permission of the authors.

THE ROUTINE

> *Got a wife and kids in Baltimore, Jack*
> *I went out for a ride and I never went back...*
> FROM "HUNGRY HEART," BY BRUCE SPRINGSTEEN

JACK MICHAELS SANG ALONG WITH THE BOSS as he drove his 1967 candy apple red Mustang convertible down the New Jersey Turnpike on the way to Newark Airport. Jack was never really a Springsteen fan until August of 1984, when his then-future wife took him to see Bruce and the E. Street Band at the Brendan Byrne Arena in East Rutherford. A few weeks ago, Jack celebrated his fiftieth birthday by attending his twenty-seventh Springsteen Concert.

> *Like a river that don't know where it's flowing*
> *I took a wrong turn and I just kept going*

Jack exited the turnpike, taking Route 81 toward the airport long-term parking lot and, as he always loved to do, put on "Born to Run," timing it so he pulled into a spot exactly as the song ended. He got out of his car, zipped up his chocolate-brown Remy leather jacket and popped open the trunk, taking out a small carry-on bag and a laptop. Jack closed the trunk and stood there, admiring his perfectly restored Mustang. He loved everything about that car from its original ragtop down to the New Jersey vanity plates with the word **"SOLD!"** printed on them.

Inside the terminal, Jesus, a TSA worker, waved Jack through security, asking where he was off to this time. Jack smiled, "Oshkosh, by gosh." Chandra, the tall Rastafarian barista at the airport Starbucks, had Jack's Caramel Macchiato ready before he even got to the register. Chandra was still bitter about the Nets moving to Brooklyn. And Jack shared her pain. He remembered how angry his father, born and raised in Flatbush, was when the Dodgers relocated to L.A. His father kept saying, "It don't take no genius to know the difference between right and wrong, and *this* bullshit is *wrong!*" Jack wondered what his old man would think about what he was doing.

On the plane, Jack grabbed an aisle seat, then faked coughing and sneezing so nobody would want the seat next to him. As usual, the ploy worked, and he had an extra seat for himself. He then opened a file on his laptop called "Leuwendyke Farm," and took a quick look at a list of farm equipment, livestock and other miscellaneous items. He usually liked to open with a joke, but this was going to be a tough crowd. Maybe an excerpt from the Bible would work better. Jack closed the laptop and lost himself in a copy of *Golf Digest*. Four hours later, his plane landed at Wittman Regional Airport in Oshkosh, Wisconsin.

Jack entered the baggage area and spotted a man dressed in black with a long beard, holding a cardboard sign saying "MICHAELS." This was Ezekiel Leuwendyke. Jack and Leuwendyke left the airport in a black horse-drawn buggy, and were soon trotting down a wooded country road. Jack, preparing himself for his performance, was busy using his laptop while his Amish driver/client looked at it with disdain.

"The first item up for bid is this hardly used handmade butter churn. Who'll give me thirty dollars? Thirty-dollar bid, thirty-dollar bid, thirty-five..." Jack, the auctioneer, was pitching to a gathering of Amish men and women at the Leuwendyke farm. "Thirty-five *once*... thirty-five *twice*... *Sold* to the man in the beard and the black hat. Next, up for bid is Ishmael, the finest plow-horse in Waupaca County." Leuwendyke led the old horse up to Jack's podium. "Blind in one eye, he'll veer a little to the left, but if you're plowing in a circle, this is the horse for you. We'll start the bidding at three hundred dollars."

Jack Michaels came from a long line of auctioneers. The gavel he used belonged to his great-grandfather, Obadiah Michaels, who, in 1865, auctioned off the tables, chairs and punchbowls that were to be used at the Confederacy's victory party. Well aware of his auctioneer heritage, Jack prided himself on being able to sell anything to anybody, and his track record bore it out. He could now add to that ten-thousand dollars worth of Amish crap.

On the buggy ride back to the airport, Jack took out his cell phone to make a call. Leuwendyke looked at the device with contempt. "Hey, Son, I'm on the way back to the airport. The clip-clops? Amish ground transportation. Tell your mom I'll be in late, not to wait up... Sure, let's do it. Why don't you book us a ten o'clock tee time for tomorrow. Love you." As soon as Jack clicked his phone off, it rang. He looked at the screen and said to Leuwendyke, "My wife." Then, "Hi, Honey. Just finished the Leuwendyke auction. I'm bringing you back a beautiful Amish quilt... What's the matter, what's wrong?... You hit 'Menu,' then 'Search,' then type in *Muppets Take Manhattan.* How difficult is that?" Jack turned to Leuwendyke, "She doesn't know how to work the TIVO." Leuwendyke shrugged. "Anyway, I'm off to Santa Fe, for the Confiscated Drug Dealers' Vehicle Auction, then Oklahoma City, for the Mickey Mantle Memorabilia Sale. Should be home next Tuesday. Love you."

"I thought you were returning home today," said Leuwendyke.

"I am," said Jack.

******

JACK'S PLANE LANDED at New York's John F. Kennedy International Airport, where he climbed into a cobalt blue 1966 Corvette Stingray convertible with New York vanity plates, also imprinted with the word **"SOLD!"** As an auctioneer, he had access to some unbelievable deals; thus the two vintage automobiles. Jack drove the Stingray up the Belt Parkway toward Long Island, this time, singing along with Billy Joel…

> *I don't care what you say anymore, this is my life*
> *Go ahead with your own life. Leave me alone…*

FLYING LADY

THE NEXT MORNING, JACK STOOD ON THE FIRST TEE at Blue View Golf Course in Massapequa, Long Island, watching his twenty-four year old son Peter tee up his ball. Jack, always meticulous in the way he dressed, especially on the golf course, sported a powder blue, silk-cotton blend Greg Norman polo shirt, tailored Ralph Lauren pants and custom-made alligator golf shoes. Peter, half a head taller than his father, was playing in jeans and a tee shirt. He was blessed with natural good looks mixed with a vulnerability many women found appealing, and some used to their advantage. Peter lined up his shot, waggled his driver three times, and crushed the ball, only to see it take a hard right and veer into the woods.

"Got dumped again, didn't you?" Jack said, as they started down the fairway.

"How'd you know?"

"Because every time you get dumped, your slice comes back. Want to talk about it?" Peter shook his head as they entered the woods to search for his ball, but Jack persisted. "Is this another one from Facebook?"

"You know what?" Peter said. "She wasn't right for me anyway. It's a good thing we never met in person."

Peter finally found a ball, realized it wasn't his, placed it back down and continued to search. "I don't want to sound like an old fart," said Jack, as he picked up the ball and pocketed it. "...but you might want to try a girl you haven't Googled."

"How else am I gonna meet anyone?" Peter said, dropping a new ball on the fairway.

"When I was your age there was no Internet," Jack said. "You had to go out into the world to meet somebody."

Peter took out his five iron, topped the ball and headed toward the first hole. Luke, a ruggedly handsome greenskeeper in his mid-forties, was on a mower, trimming the fairway around the green. He pulled to the side and shut the engine as Jack chipped onto the putting surface, his ball landing a foot from the hole. "Nice shot, Mr. Michaels."

"I'll be out of your way in a second, Luke," Peter shouted from just off the green.

"Take your time, son," said Luke. He watched Peter skull his shot over the green, then trudge after it.

Jack filled Luke in. "Girl problems."

"He didn't get anybody knocked up, did he? 'Cause those condoms, they can break on you."

"He never gets that far."

Actually, Peter had gotten that far plenty of times, but unlike most hot-blooded, young males, he found sex for sex's sake unfulfilling. His problem wasn't attracting girls, it was attracting the right girl — one who will love you, even though you're on a teacher's salary and still live with your parents.

Jack and Peg Michaels moved into their ranch style house on the edge of the eighth fairway when Blue View Country Club first opened, over twenty-eight years ago. Jack had grown up in Brooklyn, surrounded by concrete, the elevated D train roaring past his window every twenty minutes drowning out the key plot points on all his favorite TV shows. He still didn't know how, like the Dodgers, Laverne and Shirley ended up in Los Angeles. Jack had vowed that one day, he'd live somewhere quiet and surrounded by grass. That's why he and Peg wound up living on a golf course. And Jack loved the game. When he wasn't on the road, he was usually out playing golf. In fact, Jack was on the eighth green when Peg went into labor with Peter. Her screams made him miss his birdie putt, but he didn't care. He wrote down a birdie on his scorecard anyway, then drove his wife in the golf cart to Massapequa Memorial.

Peter grew up wanting to be just like his dad, and by the age of five he was auctioning off his toys to the other kids. Young Peter idolized his father, and cherished the little time Jack spent at home because he was on the road so much. He often begged his father to take him along on one of his business trips, but Jack never would, telling his son that auctioneering was a tough life. "You have to be away from your wife, your kids, eat lousy food, sleep in rundown motels. The last thing I want is for you to be like me. Do something you love."

Peter took his father's advice and decided to become a cowboy, but changed his mind at his eighth birthday party after being thrown from a rented pony. His next choices were professional wrestler, concert pianist, and ventriloquist. But he had no wrestling skills or musical talent, and the first dummy he bought scared the heck out of him. So, he settled on President of the United States.

He was only eleven when he began reading everything he could get his hands on about the U.S. Presidency. Peter soon discovered he wasn't just reading about George Washington, he was learning about the American Revolution and the creation of the United States Constitution. When he was reading about Theodore Roosevelt, he found himself immersed in the building of the Panama Canal. And when he read about Richard Nixon, the events of Watergate topped any fiction he'd ever come across. Peter eventually realized it was history he loved, not the Oval Office. Besides, having the fate of the world in your hands seemed like way too much responsibility for an eleven-year-old. So, he gave up the Presidency and decided to become a history teacher.

On this particular afternoon, Peter sat at the backyard patio table with an iPad, while Jack used a net to fish errant golf balls from the pool, dumping them into a large bucket. Four Callaways, six Pinnacles, two Top-Flites and a Srixon. Not a bad haul for the two weeks he'd been away. Jack hadn't paid for a golf ball in years.

Peter's mother, Peg, emerged from the house in a floral print sundress, wearing a hand-made bonnet Jack had brought back from the Amish auction. Jack first met Peg on a hot August day, after she was runner up in the 1985 Miss Jones Beach contest. He had taken a picture of her with his Polaroid camera and handed it to her when she stepped off the stage. Now just shy of fifty, Peg had retained her good looks and could still almost fit in the swimsuit she wore that day.

"Peter, do I look like Kelly McGillis in *Witness*?"

"What's '*Witness*?'" Peter asked, transfixed on his iPad.

"That movie with Harrison Ford," explained Jack. "Before he was shtupping that Ally McBeal."

"Shtupping?" asked Peg.

"Amish expression," said Jack. "Anything happen while I was away?

"Walter Morgan was elected president of the club."

"Walter Morgan?! That idiot wants to make the greens ten-five on the stimpmeter. Even worse, he's threatened to change the Bloody Mary mix in the clubhouse. And those free honey roasted peanuts I fought so hard for? They're not gonna be free anymore! To hell with Walter Morgan!" shouted Jack, as he stormed into the house.

Peter looked up from his iPad. "Should I put down my favorite cheese is Gouda?"

"You're not doing another profile, are you?" asked his mother.

Peter was convinced this was the dating site for him. After all, Ted Crane, the chemistry teacher, got dates from this site and half his face was charred from a Bunsen Burner accident. Peg wished Peter good luck and went into the house as he continued creating his profile on Datefinder.com:

> *I'm a twenty-four year old history teacher from Massapequa, Long Island. I like to read, play golf and eat sushi. I'm into fitness, but not obsessed. A little flab doesn't scare me. In fact my last date listed her weight as*

CRASH! A pink golf ball smashed into the iPad. Peter picked up the ball and walked toward the fence bordering the golf course. On the other side, an attractive young woman, in her early twenties, came toward him. She had brown hair, hazel eyes and was carrying a seven iron.

"Did you see a Flying Lady?" she asked, somewhat sheepishly.

"You mean the one that just hit my iPad?" Peter showed her the cracked screen, then handed her the ball.

"I'm sorry. I've been fighting a hook all day."

"Don't worry about it. When you live on a golf course, it comes with the territory."

"I know. I live on a golf course, too. Our schnauzer was in a coma for two weeks after getting struck by a Titleist."

"Damn. Is he okay?"

"He is. Except now, every time somebody yells 'fore,' he puts his paws over his head." She put her hands over her head to mimic the dog. He laughed, then noticed the name, "Quail Brook," on her visor.

"Is Quail Brook your home course?"

"Yes, in Somerset, New Jersey."

This girl was too good to be true; she played golf, had a sense of humor, and was smokin' hot. "Hey, Beth, drop a ball and hit!" yelled a good-looking guy walking up the fairway.

"Boyfriend?" Peter asked.

"Gay friend," she said. "We go to culinary school together."

"Wow, you're going to be a chef. I eat food."

She laughed. "What a coincidence. Look, I insist on paying." She wrote down her cell phone number on a scorecard and told him to let her know what it cost to repair his screen. She then dropped her ball and got ready to hit.

"Whoa, whoa, wait. You're completely closed," Peter said. "Open your left foot a little."

She adjusted her stance and swung. The ball landed ten feet from the pin.

"Nice shot, Beth," said Peter.

Beth smiled, "Thanks for the tip..."

Peter smiled back, "Peter... Peter Michaels."

"Really? My last name's Michaels, too," she said as she started down the fairway. "If we got married, I wouldn't have to change it." He watched her walk all the way to the green.

******

The next morning Peter and his parents were at the breakfast table, Peter on the phone with the Apple Store Tech Support.

"This sausage tastes funny," complained Jack.

"It's not sausage, it's Tofurkey," Peg explained. "You know what Dr. Schlesinger said about your cholesterol."

"Schlesinger can Tofuckhimself. Give this crap to the dog."

"We don't have a dog."

"If we had one."

Peter ended his call. "I can get the screen fixed for eighty-nine bucks. Maybe I shouldn't bother her."

"Did that golf ball hit you in the head?" said Jack. "This is what I've been talking about. That ball could have landed anywhere, but it found *you*. Call her. Ask her out, person to person."

THE JUMP

Peter had just finished teaching history to a ninth grade class and was sitting in his empty classroom. He'd only been teaching for three years, but had already established a reputation as the teacher kids want to have, the kind that makes a difference in a student's life. He was tireless in his preparation and was constantly coming up with innovative ways to make history come alive. Today, for his lesson on the Cold War, Peter dressed up as Russian Premier Khrushchev, bald cap and all. His students especially loved when he banged on the desk with his shoe, shouting, "We will bury you!"

Morbidly obese gym teacher, Lenny Stokes, entered the classroom, a whistle around his neck and a carton of cigarettes under his arm. "Hey, Nikita, look what I found in Eddie Nicholson's book bag," he said, holding up the cigarettes.

"Good, you confiscated them," said Peter.

"Of course I did. They're my brand."

"I thought you gave up smoking because of your father."

"So he's got lung cancer. He's got a big dick, too. I didn't get that."

Lenny and Peter first met when they were assigned roommates at Stony Brook University. When Peter walked into their dorm room for the first time, he found Lenny naked on his back, trying to give himself a blowjob. He pinched a nerve in his neck and Peter had to take him to the infirmary where Lenny wrote down the "cause of accident" as "small dick." Lenny was an acquired taste and Peter wasn't sure he'd fully acquired that taste yet. But there was something about Lenny that Peter found comforting. What you saw was what you got — a disgusting, loyal friend.

"What are you doing tonight?" Lenny asked, scratching his crotch.

"The same thing I always do," replied Peter. "Lesson plans and marking papers. And there's an Eli Whitney documentary on the History Channel."

"Fuck Eli Whitney," said Lenny. "They're opening up a new strip club in Westbury." He handed Peter a coupon. "We each get a free lap dance."

"I'm a teacher. I cannot be seen in a strip club."

"It's always about you, isn't it? Fine, I'll go myself." Lenny started to leave.

"Wait a second, aren't you coaching a game tonight against Hempstead?"

"I called and forfeited. What's the difference? We stink anyway." Lenny popped a cigarette in his mouth and headed out.

*****

At the Jean Claude Culinary Academy in Manhattan, Beth and her friend Phil were among a group of twenty culinary students, each in front of their own cooking station complete with stove, oven and prep area. Instructor Chef Wong informed the students they had three minutes left to complete their dishes before Executive Chef Jean Claude was to arrive.

When Beth was five, her parents gave her an Easy Bake oven for Hanukkah. To their surprise, on the eighth night she baked a cheesecake to die for; another Hanukkah miracle. From that day on, she wanted to become a chef.

It was the moment of truth as Chef Jean Claude conducted his taste test. Voted Sexiest Chef of the Year by *Bon Appétit* Magazine, and whose restaurant, Le Canard, was the recipient of two Michelin stars, Chef Jean Claude could be as blunt as a dull knife. "Beth, your soufflé is as lovely as you are. It's going on the menu. Phil, your soufflé is going in the garbage." Then he dumped it in the trash and left.

"He hates me," Phil sighed.

Beth put her arm around him. "He doesn't hate *you*, he hates your *soufflé*." Her cell phone buzzed. "Hello... Peter who? Oh, the guy who cured my hook."

Peter, still in his Khrushchev bald cap, was in his empty classroom on the cell phone. He told Beth he was calling about the iPad bill. She asked for his address so she could send him a check. Peter hesitated. He remembered back when he was six-years-old and climbed up the high diving board at the club. Upon reaching the top, he looked down and became terrified, screaming for his dad to rescue him, but Jack was at the snack shop, talking to a woman in a bikini. Scared to death, Peter closed his eyes and jumped.

Peter closed his eyes and jumped. "I was wondering if you could give it to me in person... like, over dinner?"

"You want me to have dinner with you?" Beth asked.

"I'm sorry, that was way too—"

"I'd love to."

"You would?!"

"On one condition: I pick the restaurant."

Maybe Peter's father was right. Maybe that ball smashing into his screen was meant to be. Peter's mind shifted into overdrive. *Is this finally the girl? Does she want children? And if so how many? I love kids, but I don't really find pregnant women attractive. What am*

I gonna wear? Should I get my teeth whitened? God, I wish I were taller. Not that I'm short. Those things aren't important to her. But what if they are? Why wouldn't she want children? I hope it's not Indian food.

SO THIS IS NEW JERSEY

THE LAST RESTAURANT PETER EXPECTED was White Castle, but there they were, wolfing down double-cheese sliders and fries. Beth explained that she spends all day in culinary school and likes to take a break from haute cuisine.

"So what was a Jersey girl doing on a Long Island golf course?" he asked.

"Phil, the guy I was playing with, his lover is Tommy McMillan, the pro at your course."

"Tommy McMillan is gay?! You know how many times he's held me from behind, adjusting my swing?"

"You're not homophobic, are you?"

"I am now."

Beth laughed. Together less than an hour, she already felt totally comfortable with Peter. Not only was he cute and funny, but he possessed the rare quality of actually listening when she talked.

New York's Chelsea Pier has the only driving range

in Manhattan. For a mere fifty dollars a bucket, golfers get to hit balls towards the Jersey side of the Hudson River. Beth and Peter warmed up by hitting a few wedges, then pulled out their drivers. Peter drove ball after ball straight down the middle, with no sign of his dreaded slice. He was pretty impressed with himself until Beth hit a prodigious tee shot, outdistancing him by about fifty yards. "What are you trying to do?" Peter asked. "Hit your house?"

"I live in Somerset, New Jersey, not Weehawken."

"I've never been there."

"Somerset, or Weehawken?"

"New Jersey."

Despite its proximity to Long Island, Peter had never set foot on New Jersey soil. His father had always said such disparaging things about the state, Peter had no desire to go there. Beth told him lots of people have a misconception about New Jersey, but it truly is the Garden State. Peter's dad called it "the Garbage State." He explained that his father was somewhat opinionated, but other than that, he was pretty cool. Both his parents were. "Is that why you still live at home?" Beth asked.

"Why, is that a problem?"

"No. Not at all. I live at home. Why pay for shit when your parents can?" she said, half joking.

Peter admitted he probably should have his own place, but on a teacher's salary, money's tight. Plus, it's really cool, living on a golf course. "And if you didn't live on that golf course..." Beth added, "I wouldn't have met you."

Beth and Peter stood on the deck of the Weehawken Ferry as it approached New Jersey. Peter never imagined anything could be so beautiful. Not New Jersey, Beth. There was a connection between them. They felt it the day they first met on the golf course. Life is funny, sometimes. If she had sliced the ball, they never would have met. The blast of the boat's whistle knocked them out of their reverie. The ferry docked, the ramp came down, and passengers began to disembark. Beth took Peter's hand and pulled him onto the dock. Peter was actually in New Jersey!

"I had a really nice time," she said.

"Me, too." Peter wanted to kiss her, but decided not to, afraid it might be too soon. "Well, I guess it's back to New York." He started to get on the boat, but Beth grabbed his arm.

"Wait, you forgot something."

"Oh, the check," Peter said.

"No, *this*," she said, pulling him to her, then pressing her lips against his.

"But what about the check?"

She pulled him back for a kiss lasting so long the ferry pulled away without him.

"My boat!" said Peter, in mid-kiss.

"There's another one at midnight." They continued

to kiss as the ferry disappeared across the river.

An hour later, Peter and Beth walked through Weehawken's Hamilton Park, on the Palisades, high above the Hudson. Peter was well aware of the park's historical significance. He pointed out that just below where the park is now, was a ledge 11 paces wide and 20 paces long. This ledge was the site of the famous duel between Alexander Hamilton, first Secretary of the Treasury, and Aaron Burr, third Vice President of the United States, which took place on July 11, 1804. She was impressed. The last guy she dated thought Roe v. Wade was Dwyane Wade's sister.

Peter and Beth sat on a bench and gazed across the river at the magnificent New York Skyline. "This is where I come when I need to think," said Beth. She told him that whenever she looks at the Empire State Building, it reminds her of the movie, *King Kong*. Peter never saw it, he wasn't into monster movies.

"It's not a monster movie," Beth said. "It's a love story."

"But, he's a gorilla." Peter argued.

"He's a metaphor for love that can never be."

"Maybe some loves aren't meant to be."

"Call me a romantic, but I believe true love can overcome any obstacle."

"But, he's a gorilla."

"All men are gorillas."

Peter beat his chest, grunted and playfully grabbed

her. They looked deeply into each other's eyes for a long moment and then, softly kissed.

WOLF BLITZER

"These eggs taste funny," complained Jack, seated at the breakfast table.

"They're not eggs," Peg explained. "They're egg substitutes."

Jack grumbled and reached for the salt, but Peg snatched it away. "You do realize I'm gonna grab some real food at the airport," Jack said.

"Don't you dare."

"What are you gonna do, follow me?"

"Maybe I will."

"All right, you win. I'll eat healthy. No need to follow me."

Jack handed Peg a brochure with pictures of wax figures up for auction at the Niagara Falls Wax Museum, which was closing due to an electrical fire that had melted half of its inventory. "Here, see if there's anyone you want me to bring back." Peg leafed through the brochure. There were wax figures of Abraham Lincoln, Britney Spears, Neil Armstrong, Abbott and Costello, and Charles de Gaulle, among the survivors.

"Oh, look, Wolf Blitzer!" squealed Peg. "He'd look absolutely stunning under our old cuckoo clock in the den." The Michaels' home was chock full of antiques Jack had brought back from years of auctioneering.

"You want him, you got him," Jack said.

Peter bounded into the kitchen, grabbing a fat-free, gluten-free, taste-free bran muffin, though the way Peter felt this morning, it was delicious.

"Remember that girl who broke my iPad? I took your advice, Dad, and went out with her. I know this is crazy, but I think I'm falling in love."

"Hallelujah!" Jack said.

"You were right, Dad. You meet people in life, not on the Internet."

"When your father and I met, there was no Internet, no texting," Peg said.

"And there was no tweeting either," Jack added. "Do I need to know if Meryl Streep just took a dump?"

"On that note..." Peter put down the muffin and headed out.

"Where you going?" Jack asked.

"We've got another date."

"A second date?" said Peg. "That's a first."

"Dad, I'll see you in... how long this time?" Peter asked.

"Two weeks," Jack said. "Niagara Falls, then Toronto, then back down to Buffalo for a B'nai Brith auction."

"I had no idea there was a Jewish community in Buffalo," Peg said.

"They're everywhere," Jack replied.

"You do realize that's an anti-Semitic statement?" Peter said.

"It's an observation."

Peter shook his head and walked out.

"He didn't even tell us her name," Jack said.

"What's the difference? Our boy is finally in love."

"Speaking of love, I don't have to leave for another hour. Wanna go upstairs for a quickie?"

"Upstairs?"

"I mean, do you want to go down the hall… to our bedroom?"

WONDERLAND

For the next two weeks, Peter and Beth spent as much time together as possible. They went to museums, an off-Broadway show, Beth's first hockey game, and Peter's first and last ballet. Mostly, they just liked to walk and talk. One day they walked the entire length of 5th Avenue, from 59th Street all the way to Washington Square in Greenwich Village, playing a game along the way. Every time they passed a street vendor, they kissed. Two kisses for a Sabrett hotdog guy. Peter and Beth grew more and more comfortable with each other, and although their physical attraction was undeniable, neither of them had a problem taking it slow.

On an Indian Summer-like morning, Peter entered Central Park through the west side at 66th Street. He crossed the park drive, making his way through hordes of weekend runners and cyclists into The Sheep Meadow, a verdant green pasture filled with picnickers, frisbee players, break dancers, artists, drum circles, folk dancers, kids playing catch, dogs playing fetch, and a man playing an oboe. Peter finally spotted Beth, waving to him from behind a group of mimes. He waved back. The mimes waved back at him. Peter and Beth approached each other, and, without saying a word, fell into an embrace, kissing passionately. So did the mimes. There were hundreds of people in the park, but it was as if no one else was there… not counting the mimes. Finally, they broke apart. So did the mimes.

"Hi," they said in unison. The mimes knew they were beaten, so they acted sad.

Peter and Beth waved goodbye to their silent friends and walked hand-in-hand through the park, stopping at the famous Alice in Wonderland sculpture to watch children play among the bronze figures of Alice, the Mad Hatter, the White Rabbit, and the Dormouse. Beth said she couldn't wait to come there with her own kids. Peter wanted kids too, but pointed out being a parent is such a responsibility. It's so easy to screw them up. "You should see some of the parents I meet on open school night," he said. "They shouldn't be allowed to have a hamster, let alone a child."

As they strolled through the Central Park's lush Conservatory Garden, they came across a wedding and sat down on a bench to watch. The bride and groom kissed. So did they. Peter pictured Beth in a beautiful, white wedding gown. She pictured him timing her contractions at Lamaze class.

They spent the rest of the day renting bicycles, visiting the Zoo, riding the carousel, and watching Met Life trounce Liberty Mutual in an inter-insurance company softball game. Before they knew it, the sun had descended, replaced by a beautiful, moonlit sky. Beth and Peter snuggled together in a horse-drawn carriage, the perfect moment for a deep, sensual kiss.

"We need to take this to the next level," Beth said, breathlessly.

"You read my mind," Peter agreed, kissing her again.

"My house in New Jersey, tomorrow."

"What about your parents?"

"I'm talking about my parents. I want you to meet them."

"Oh."

The next morning, Peter was in the family driveway, washing his blue 2008 Honda Accord while his mother looked on.

"Meeting her parents, that's big," Peg said.

Peter was apprehensive about meeting Beth's parents. Peg assured him there was nothing to be nervous about. "If they don't like you, something's wrong with them."

"Did your parents like Dad the first time they met him?"

"My father did, but your Grandma Lucy thought he was a smoothie because he gave her a watch."

"Then I probably shouldn't give Beth's mother this car," Peter said.

Peg kissed his cheek. "It's nice to see you so happy."

"Thanks, Mom."

"So, when do we get to meet Beth?"

"Maybe when Dad gets back from Buffalo. I'll bring her home for dinner. But I'm warning you, she's studying to be a chef, so you better be on your game."

"Now, *I'm* nervous," she laughed.

HER DADDY

You know she thrills me with all her charms,
When I'm wrapped up in my baby's arms
My little angel gives me everything
I know someday that she'll wear my ring.

So don't bother me 'cause I got no time
I'm on my way to see that girl of mine,
Nothin' else matters in this whole wide world,
When you're in love with a Jersey girl,

FROM "JERSEY GIRL" BY TOM WAITS

PETER DROVE DOWN THE JERSEY TURNPIKE on his way to Beth's house, passing oil refineries, power plants, and industrial smoke stacks. *Dad was wrong*, thought Peter. *New Jersey is beautiful.* Six tolls later, he exited the turnpike and took the Memorial Parkway past New Brunswick, finally arriving in the town of Somerset, which as Peter had researched, was famous for two things — it housed one of the first Marconi

Wireless Radio Stations in America, and it was the home of Randall Pinkett, winner of season four of *The Apprentice*.

Peter's car turned onto a local street, passing the entrance to Quail Brook Country Club. He parked in an open spot, crossed the street to a two story house and rang the bell. Beth's mother, an attractive woman in her mid-forties, opened the door. Peter's father always told him, *if you want to know what a girl is going to look like in twenty years, take a look at her mother.* Peter thought that was a shallow statement, bordering on sexist, but right now he was okay with it. "Mrs. Michaels?" he asked.

"Please, 'Rebecca.' Come in, Peter."

He walked into a tastefully decorated living room filled with mostly antiques, and was immediately greeted by Lucky, the family schnauzer. Peter knelt down and scratched him behind his ears.

"That's a good sign," Rebecca said. "He usually doesn't take to strangers. Come on, Lucky, let's show Peter the house." She took Peter's arm and gave him the grand tour. "Did you have any trouble getting here?"

"No, but I almost got arrested for pumping my own gas."

Rebecca laughed. "In 1949, New Jersey made it illegal to pump your own gas. It was deemed too dangerous to have untrained people dispensing such a flammable liquid. How do I know? I teach Social

Studies at Somerset High."

"History, Massapequa High," said Peter.

"Well then, we have something in common."

Rebecca took him into the back yard, bordering the seventh fairway of Quail Brook, where Peter noticed they had another thing in common. The swimming pool, like Peter's, had a bucket next to it, containing errant golf balls. Rebecca and Peter walked back into the house as Beth came down from her bedroom.

"What do you think, Mom?" Beth asked, putting her arm through Peter's.

"He's a babe, alright," Rebecca said.

"I hope your husband feels the same way," Peter said. "I mean, I hope he likes me."

"You'll find out soon enough," Beth said. "He's on his way home from the airport. Come on, let's hang in my room till he gets here."

As soon as they entered her room, Beth pushed Peter onto the bed and jumped on top of him, showering him with kisses. "So, do you like my mom?"

"God, I like your mom," Peter said, as they continued making out.

"If you like her, you're gonna love my dad."

"I think I love this whole family. Is it too soon to ask you to marry me?"

"You're just saying that because you have an erection."

She heard a car pull into the driveway. "Daddy!!!"

"*Had* an erection," muttered Peter.

They got off the bed and quickly straightened their clothes. Suddenly, Peter was shaking. Beth's father's approval was important to him. Beth said not to worry, "Dad's a great guy."

Beth and Peter came down the living room stairs. The front door opened, and in walked PETER'S FATHER!!! Beth ran to him and gave him a big hug. "Daddy, this is Peter." All the blood rushed from Peter's head as he hit the canvas.

DANCER'S LEGS

Peter, unconscious, was flat out on the living room couch, his father sitting next to him. Peter's eyes opened. "Dad, I had the weirdest dream. I was at my new girlfriend's house in New Jersey and you were her father. How crazy is that? You never go to New Jersey."

Beth entered from the kitchen carrying an ice pack. "How's he doing, Daddy?"

Jack quickly put his hand over Peter's mouth. "He's still out. Go get the smelling salts from my bathroom. Hurry!" She ran upstairs. Jack removed his hand.

"*Your* bathroom?!" said a stunned Peter.

"How is he, Jacob?" Rebecca said, coming out of the kitchen.

"*Jacob*?!" Peter asked.

Jack quickly put his hand over Peter's mouth.

"Why are you covering his mouth?" asked Rebecca.

"I'm making him breathe through his nose," said

Jack. "Better yet, I'll take him for a drive in the convertible. The fresh air will do him good."

Jack rushed the bewildered Peter out the front door and shoved him into the passenger seat of his red Mustang convertible, the one with Jersey plates, then backed the car out of the driveway and sped off. "What the hell's going on?!" Peter said, finally able to string some words together.

"Look, this is not something that's easy to explain."

"Try."

"Okay, here goes. Back in the Eighties, I was the auctioneer at a fund raiser for the Somerset school system. Rebecca was assigned to help me. We spent three straight days working closely together and raised enough money to establish a breakfast program for disadvantaged students, as well as glass backboards for all the school gyms. Rebecca was vivacious, intelligent, and had dancer's legs. Call me weak, but I fell in love with her. At the same time, I didn't fall out of love with your mother."

"You're a bigamist!" Peter shouted.

"I am *not* a *bigamist*," Jack protested. "I just have two wives and two families who I love and provide for equally. I dare you to tell me you haven't had a good life up until now."

Peter shook his head in disbelief. "I finally meet the girl of my dreams, and she turns out to be my sister."

"I *told* you to stay out of New Jersey," said Jack.

"I didn't meet her in New Jersey! I met her in our backyard! Remember?!"

"I need coffee," muttered Jack. He pulled into a Starbucks parking lot and headed inside, Peter chasing after him. Jack ordered a Grande Caramel Macchiato for himself and a Vanilla Venti Latte for his son.

"I love her," said Peter.

"If you love her, then you'll protect our secret," whispered Jack.

"*Our* secret?!"

"Yes, *our* secret. And keep it down. I live in this community."

Jack took their drinks and searched for a place to sit. All the tables were taken by the usual suspects—iPaders, and laptoppers who had ordered their coffees three hours ago, and had nothing better to do with their lives, so they were still there.

"Jacob!" Jack turned to see a middle-aged man wearing a Quail Brook golf hat approach. "I've got two seats over there with Ira and Mel," said the man. Two of Jack's golfing buddies waved from a table across the room.

"Thanks, Barry, but we got these to go."

"Aren't you going to introduce me, *Jacob*?" said Peter.

"Uh… Barry Brodsky, this is Peter, my, uh… "

"Daughter's *boyfriend*," Peter said, pointedly.

"You're a lucky man, Peter," Barry said. "Beth is quite a catch. You know, my son, Alan, took her to the

Senior Prom. Jacob, remember how worried you were he might try something?"

"Did he?!" asked Peter.

"Did *you*?!" asked Jack.

On the way back to the house, Peter started to piece everything together. No wonder every Thanksgiving Jack would insist on an early afternoon turkey dinner and then leave for his annual Thanksgiving Day poker game. There was no poker game. He was in New Jersey, eating Beth's mother's stuffing.

"I didn't want anyone to feel left out," Jack explained.

"What about Christmas?"

"I don't have to be here on Christmas. On this side of the Hudson, I'm a Jew."

"But you always say such terrible things about the Jews."

"So nobody gets suspicious. I love the Jews. I'm married to one."

They pulled into the driveway and it started to drizzle. "Peter, I know this is hard for you to understand," Jack said, putting up the convertible top. "But if the truth comes out, everyone will get hurt, especially your mother. If you told her about this it would destroy her. Do you want that on your conscience? I sure don't. I love that woman more than anyone else in the world." Rebecca and Beth came out of the house holding umbrellas. "Except for them. And you."

"You're insane," Peter said, as they got out of the car.

Beth ran up to Peter. "Are you alright?"

"I'm okay," he said, shooting daggers at his dad."

"Well, come inside before it pours." She put her arm through his, making him extremely uncomfortable. After all, she was his sister.

"Listen, I'm sorry, everybody," Peter said. "But I'm gonna go home and get into bed."

"Good idea," said Jack.

"Bad idea," said Beth. "There's a terrible storm on the way and he just fainted. Peter, you're sleeping here."

"I'll drive him home," said Jack.

"Jacob, you are not a good driver in the rain," argued Rebecca. "Remember Hawaii? You crashed into that pineapple stand and broke your arm."

"When was this?" Peter asked.

"Three years ago at Kapalua," Rebecca said. "We went with our temple."

"What a coincidence," Peter said. "My dad broke his arm three years ago, too. He slipped on the ice in Chicago while he was on one of his 'business trips.'"

"What does your father do?" Rebecca asked.

Before Peter could answer, there was a loud clap of thunder and it started to pour.

"Let's go inside, before we get drenched," said Beth. The two women rushed into the house.

"Please," Jack begged.

"Blow me," shot back Peter.

"Hey, I'm still your father," snapped Jack, as they entered the house.

"Everybody, I have something to say," announced Peter. Jack glared at him.

Just then a fourteen-year-old boy in a wheelchair rolled into the room. "Will somebody help me take my fucking pants off?"

"Todd, what did we tell you about that language?" Rebecca said. "Go to your room, now."

"Yes, Mom." Todd wheeled himself away.

"You'll have to excuse Todd," Rebecca said. "His whole life, he's been bounced from foster home to foster home."

"Daddy found out about him from our Rabbi and decided to adopt him," Beth said, putting her arms around her dad and kissing him on the cheek. "Aren't I lucky to have such a wonderful father?"

"And husband," Rebecca added.

Jack put his arms around his adoring girls, painting a perfect family picture. Peter was defeated.

"Where do I sleep?"

It was 2:00 A.M. in the family guest room. Peter, in boxer shorts, was unable to sleep. He got off the bed and looked at some framed pictures on the dresser. There was a wedding photo of Peter's father, wearing a yarmulke, next to his bride, Rebecca. A snapshot of his father, Rebecca, and five-year-old Beth on the beach at the Jersey shore, as well as a family photo with his father, Rebecca and Beth, all gathered around Todd in his wheelchair, as he blew out the candles on a birthday cake. Peter picked up the family photo and stared at it, lost in thought. The door opened. Beth, wearing a robe, sneaked in and hugged him from behind, reaching into the front of his boxers. Peter jumped! "What are you doing?!"

"What do you think I'm doing?"

"Let go!" He moved away.

"Peter, a little while ago you were all over me."

"That's before I knew."

"Knew what?"

"That you're... you're..." He then noticed the Star of David around her neck. "... a Jew."

"What?!"

"You heard me. I was raised in a good Christian household."

"What is that supposed to mean?"

"It means I was raised a certain way. Like they taught me the difference between Jews and canoes."

"And that is?"

"Canoes tip."

"That's not funny, Peter."

"Say that again?"

"That's not funny."

"I wonder how that sounded before?"

"Before what?"

"The nose job. You people all get them."

"I can't believe I'm hearing this."

Peter couldn't believe he was saying this, but what choice did he have? Rebecca entered in her robe and pajamas and asked if everything was okay. "Hey, Mrs. Michaels," Peter said. "How come none of you Jewish mothers are on parole boards?"

"I have no idea."

"You never let anyone finish a sentence."

"That's not true."

"Did you hear about the Jewish dilemma? Free pork!"

Beth had heard enough. "That's it. Get out!" she screamed.

Jack came out of his bedroom wearing pajamas as Beth was shoving Peter through the door. "What's going on?"

"Peter hates us because we're Jewish," cried Beth.

"I hate you the most," Peter said, glaring at his father.

"I'll take care of this anti-Semite," said Jack. He gave Peter the bum's rush down the stairs. Peter's pants, shirt and shoes came flying down after him.

It was still pouring outside as Jack and Peter emerged from the house. "Jew jokes. Brilliant," said Jack.

"Guess who I learned them from?" scowled Peter, crossing the street. "And don't think you're in the clear, because you're not!" Peter threw his clothes into his car and drove away, leaving his father standing in the rain.

SECRETS

It was Monday morning in Massapequa and the aroma of bacon and eggs wafted through the Michaels' house. Jack and his high cholesterol were out of town. Peter dragged himself into the kitchen looking like a guy who just found out his father has been leading a double life for twenty-five years and his girlfriend is now his sister. "I heard you come in late last night," said his mother, at the stove. "I guess things went well?"

"I don't want to talk about it," Peter said, slumping into a chair.

"What's wrong?"

"What's wrong is, you think people are one thing, and they're not."

Peg assumed he was talking about Beth. As usual, Mom was supportive. "Sweetheart, if she's not the one, I'm sure someone else will come along."

"I'm not talking about her."

"Then who are you talking about?"

"Nobody. Forget I said anything. Can I just have some eggs?"

To his surprise, she let it go, but he couldn't. "Mom, did Dad ever take you on one of his business trips?

"No, none I can think of."

"Don't you get lonely while he's away?"

"Yes," said Peg, shaking way too much pepper into the eggs. "But when two people love each other, you do everything you can to make it work, no matter how hard."

"And you never keep secrets from each other?"

"Peter, what are you getting at? What are you trying to say?"

"Nothing, Mom, nothing." Peter got up. "I'm not hungry." He headed out of the kitchen. As soon as he was gone, Peg took a bottle of vodka from the cabinet and poured herself a stiff one.

******

JACK WAS IN AN EMERGENCY SESSION with his therapist, Dr. Lorenzo Salvatore, who was still in his tennis clothes. He saw Dr. Salvatore because, every so often, he felt guilty about what he was doing. "We knew something like this would eventually happen," said Dr. Salvatore.

"No, *you* knew," snapped Jack. "*I* was doing *fine* until that stupid tee shot hit my son's iPad. A fortune in golf lessons, and she still hooks the ball."

"We have an additional problem now, don't we?" said Salvatore.

"What?"

"Your son is in love with your daughter."

"Oh yeah, that."

"Yes, Jack… that."

******

The next day, Peter sat at his teacher's desk struggling to focus as fourteen-year-old Brittany gave her report. "Although his term was cut short by an assassin's bullet, John F. Kennedy is still considered one of the greatest presidents our country has ever had."

"Sure, if you don't count all his cheating," muttered Peter.

"What do you mean, Mr. Michaels?" Brittany asked.

"Hello? Marilyn Monroe? Judith Campbell Exner? Kennedy makes Bill Clinton look like a choir boy. I'm not saying he deserved to be shot in the head…" The kids looked at their teacher like he was crazy.

✶✶✶✶✶✶

In 2012 Jack, a.k.a. Jacob, was voted "Mensch of the Year" by the board of directors of Temple Emanuel in Somerset. That year, he raised over $15,000 at the synagogue's Purim auction. He also adopted Todd after seven Jewish families gave him back, the last one claiming he set their Sukkah on fire. Jack, wearing a plaid yarmulke, was in the shul, spilling the beans to Rabbi Feldman, who couldn't believe what he was hearing. "And you've been doing this for how long?" asked the Rabbi.

"Twenty-five, give or take a year," answered Jack.

"Oy, gevalt. And the Long Island one's a Shiksa?"

"Catholic. And so am I when I'm over there."

"Jesus, my head is spinning like a dreidel."

"My son hates me, my daughter's miserable. What do I do, Rabbi?"

"Have you considered telling Rebecca the truth?"

"I bare my soul to you with my problem, and your answer is to tell the truth?!"

Jack suspected that Rabbi Feldman had an ulterior motive. He was only advising Jack to come clean to Rebecca so *he* could have a shot at her. Jack had seen how Feldman stared at Rebecca during Saturday services — how he couldn't keep his eyes off her legs when she was sitting shiva for her father. Jack angrily removed his yarmulke. "I'm going to see my priest!"

Jack and Peg had been members of Saint Cecelia Catholic Church ever since they moved to Massapequa. Last year, he donated enough money to put in a new stained glass window behind the altar. Jack was now in the confession booth seeking absolution from Father McKenzie. "Bless me, Father, for I have sinned."

"You've been sinning for twenty-five years," said the old priest. What's changed?"

"My son and my daughter met and fell in love."

"Well, they're not getting married in this church."

"Don't worry Father, nobody's getting married, but I need your advice. How can I put the fear of God into my son, so he keeps his mouth shut?

"Peter knows your disgusting secret?"

"So does Rabbi Feldman. I finally told him."

"Let me guess, he made you feel guilty."

"He said I should tell my wife the truth."

"Well, don't you think it's time you did?"

The priest believed Peter finding out about Jack's double life was no accident. It was a message from God. The only chance at salvation was to go home and tell Peg the truth. Otherwise Jack was going straight to Hell. Jack said, "I spend half my time as a Jew, and we don't believe in Hell. Thanks for nothing, Father." Jack slammed shut the little window and stormed out of the confession booth.

Next stop, Peter's school, to make sure he was still with the program.

At Massapequa High, Lenny was addressing Peter's History class. "First of all, I'd like to dispel the rumor that Mr. Michaels had a nervous breakdown. He's probably just sick of you kids. I know I am. Anyway, given that this is a history class, who can tell me who invented the jockstrap?"

"We're supposed to be learning about the Louisiana Purchase," said a freckle-faced girl in the third row.

"See, this is why I'm sick of you," said Lenny. Just then, he noticed Peter's father standing outside the classroom door, trying to get his attention. "Class, I'll be right back. Meanwhile, I brought this from my locker. Pass it around." He handed one of the students an old jockstrap and joined Jack in the hallway. "Hey, Mr. Michaels. Wazzup?"

"Where's Peter?"

"I'm covering for him. He said he needed to go home."

"Shit!"

Jack dashed out. He needed to get home too, before Peg got back from her Tuesday golf league and Peter ratted him out.

******

LUKE, THE GREENSKEEPER, shirtless in the warm afternoon sun, was planting flowers on the fifteenth tee box at Blue View Golf Course.

Peg and three of her girlfriends, Eileen, Allison and Sandy, rode up in golf carts. He politely greeted them and went back to his work. On the tee, Allison admitted to having fantasies about Luke ever since the time she saw him aerating the short par three on the back nine wearing only cargo shorts.

"I think about him too," Sandy said. "I mean look at those pecs."

"Are we playing golf or ogling the maintenance people?" Peg said.

"Ogling," Sandy said. "Have you seen my husband with his shirt off? He's got bigger breasts than I do."

Peg hit her drive in the middle of the fairway. As she bent down to pick up her tee she noticed Luke staring at her. He quickly looked away.

"My turn," said Allison, purposely giving Luke a good view of her rear as she teed up her ball.

"Stop flirting and hit the damn ball," Peg snarled.

******

PETER WAS IN THE FAMILY ROOM, light-gun in hand, playing a video game when Jack entered. "Peter, I was just at your school. Why did you come home?"

"Aren't you supposed to be in Buffalo or Des Moines or wherever the hell you're supposed to be when you're really in a house on some New Jersey cul-de-sac going down on a woman who is not my mother?" said Peter.

"You make it sound so ugly."

"You want ugly? Here's ugly. I was this close to fucking my sister."

"Technically your half-sister," said Jack.

"*Die*, you bigamist!" Peter shouted, obliterating a zombie on the screen.

"You haven't said anything to your mother, have you?"

"Not yet. It depends on if I win this video game or not. If I were you, I'd root for the Zombies."

Jack's cell phone rang. The caller ID showed "Rebecca," so he went into the kitchen, out of Peter's earshot. Rebecca was under the impression that Jack was in Buffalo for the B'nai Brith auction. "Hi, Honey," Jack said. "Just got in an hour ago. Remind me never to live here."

Rebecca told Jack she was calling because Beth was still deeply depressed about Peter. "I don't know who raised that boy, but I'd like to tell them a thing or two." Beth got on the phone and told her father she didn't understand. Peter seemed so wonderful, how could he be a Jew hater?

"That's why we can never forget," said Jack. "But you can forget this hate monger. There are plenty of nice guys out there."

"Where?" she implored.

"I don't know, look on the Internet." Just then, Jack

glanced out the window and saw Peg pulling up in her golf cart. He quickly knocked on the table, telling Beth it was room service and he had to go. He hung up just as Peter came in from the living room.

"Guess what, Jacob. Zombies lose and so do you."

Peg entered from the garage. "Jack, what are you doing back from Buffalo? And Peter, why aren't you in school?"

"I got my dates wrong. B'nai Brith is next week. And Peter left his lesson plans at home."

Before Peter could counter his father's lie, the doorbell rang. It was Walter Morgan. Jack assumed he was there to brag about becoming club president, but the reason Walter was there was to inform Jack and Peg they'd been voted Blue View Country Club's Couple of the Year. Peter was astonished. "Couple of the Year?"

"Finally!" said Peg.

"How? He's never home." asked Peter.

"That's what I said," muttered Walter. "Anyway, there's going to be a dinner in your honor on the fourteenth."

Jack acted like he was excited, but in reality, he couldn't have cared less. He'd already been Couple of the Year with Rebecca at Quail Brook, twice. But Peg was overjoyed. "Thank you, Walter. And thank you, my darling husband." She kissed Jack, who smiled angelically at Peter. "I've got to go call the girls," said Peg, happily scurrying into the kitchen.

"It's not all good news, Jack," said Walter, on his way out. "I changed the Bloody Mary mix. And peanuts are three dollars a bowl."

Peter was visibly shaken, not about the peanuts, but about what had just transpired.

"You can't tell her now, can you?" said Jack, "It'll destroy her."

Peter stood there in frustrated silence. "You're doing the right thing, son. Perhaps in time, you and I can work things out and we can resume the wonderful relationship we had before I got caught. How about a round of golf next week?"

"Only if you let me beat you to death with my sand wedge."

******

Peter's compliance sparked renewed vigor and enthusiasm in Jack about continuing his double life. He even started thinking ahead about how he would pull off retirement. Tucson and Scottsdale looked doable, or maybe West Palm Beach and Boca Raton. Everything could work out. It all depended on Peter keeping the secret… for the rest of his life. Or at least Jack's.

RUNNING WITH THE BULLS

Luke, the greenskeeper, sat in a golf cart near the sixteenth fairway at the Blue View Golf Course, watching Peter line up his shot. Peter looked like he hadn't slept in weeks, because he hadn't. "Kind of late, isn't it?" Luke asked.

"This is the only time you can play by yourself," Peter said.

"I already pulled the flag. Hole's ten feet left of the bunker."

"Thanks."

"Are you okay?"

"I'll be all right. I just have to work some things out."

"Well, I'll leave you to hit your shot." Luke started to drive off, then stopped. "Hey, if you ever want to have a beer, and just sit and shoot the breeze sometime…"

"Yeah, sounds cool," Peter said, politely.

Peter hit his ball and headed up the fairway. On the green, he lined up his shot and putted, missing the hole by a foot.

"You moved your head." Peter looked up and saw Beth standing on the green.

"Your mom told me you'd be here."

"You went to my house?"

"That sweet woman did not teach her child to hate."

"Yeah, well, you haven't met my father."

"There's a reason you broke up with me, and it's not because of my religion."

"We just don't belong together," said Peter.

She walked over to him, needing to know the truth. "Look at me. Tell me you don't love me."

"I can't."

"Then why don't you want us to be together?"

Peter hadn't inherited his father's penchant for lying and seeing what it was doing to Beth was unbearable, so despite the possible ramifications for his mother, he made a difficult decision.

"I need to show you something."

A little later, Peter and Beth entered through the front door of the Michaels' house. Peg came in from the kitchen, hoping the two of them could work out whatever it was that had come between them. To give them a chance to be alone, Peg said she was running over to the clubhouse for Bloody Mary night.

"Your father hates the new mix, Peter. But, he's in Cleveland, so while the cat's away…"

"What a coincidence," Beth said. "My father's in Cleveland."

"Hold that thought," Peter said. "Mom, have a good time." And Peg left.

"She's so nice," Beth said. "I love your mom."

"So does your dad."

"What?!"

Peter took Beth into the living room, sat her down next to him on the sofa and pulled out a family album. He turned to a photo of Peg in a hospital bed, holding her newborn baby.

"Is that you?" Beth said. "You're so cute. And your mom is so pretty."

"Look at the guy next to her."

"Your dad?" Suddenly, she realized she was looking at *her* father. "Oh my God!"

Peter turned the page. Now, it was a picture of Beth's father holding baby Peter, in church at his Christening. Then, a photo of her father showing five-year-old Peter how to hit a nerf golf ball. Next, a snapshot of her father with Peter on his shoulders, standing with Peg in the ocean at Jones Beach.

"He's had two families for twenty-five years," Peter said.

"My poor mother," Beth said, fighting back tears.

"I found out the day I came to your house,"

Peter said. "He made me promise not to blow his cover. Too many people would get hurt."

"I knew you didn't hate me because I'm Jewish."

"Hate you? I love you."

"I love you, too."

They embraced, then, realizing, she pushed him away.

"You're my brother!"

"Yeah, and it's killing me."

"How could he do this to us?" Beth picked up the family album and continued leafing through it.

"That's me and 'Dad' running with the bulls in Pamplona," said Peter. "He got gored pretty bad."

"Was this four years ago?"

"Yes."

"He told us he got stabbed chasing a mugger in Detroit."

"Guess what? He lied."

"Hello? I'm back from Cleveland." They looked up as Jack, suitcase in hand, unwittingly walked into the living room. He was trapped.

"How could you?" cried Beth.

"How could I what, Sweetheart?" said Jack, trying to come off like he hadn't stumbled into a hornets' nest.

"Stop it!" she shouted.

Jack went over to the window and stared out into the darkness. This was his little girl in so much pain. At the very least, he owed her an explanation.

"I didn't wake up one day and say, 'I think I'll have two families. That'll be neat. That'll be fun.' It just happened. And once it did, I got in so deep, I couldn't get out. But please, understand, I never meant to hurt anybody. I love you all."

Peg entered from outside. "I am so stupid. Bloody Mary night is tomorrow." Then seeing her husband, "Jack, you're back!"

"Caught an early flight," he said, trying to stay calm.

"I see you've met Beth," she said. "Don't they make a wonderful couple?"

"And so do you," said Beth, fighting back tears as she bolted out the front door.

"She's upset because we're not getting back together," Peter said, running out after her.

"I don't think they're right for each other," said Jack.

Outside, Peter found Beth across the street in her car, sobbing over the steering wheel. He opened the door. "Move over, I'm driving you home."

On the drive to New Jersey, Beth was getting over the shock and her mood had transitioned from sorrow to anger. "I don't care what kind of deal you made with him, my mother deserves to know."

"What about her heart condition?"

"What heart condition?"

"Oh, he's good," Peter said.

"*Was* good," she countered. "This charade is over."

Peter admired her. She had the guts to do what he couldn't.

THE PROPOSAL

IT WAS LATE AFTERNOON in the Michaels' kitchen on Long Island. Peg was calmly doing the crossword puzzle while Jack's insides were churning, afraid of what Beth might do.

"Famous fibber, nine letters?" Peg asked.

"Pinocchio," Jack said. "I'm gonna go clean my golf shoes in the garage."

Rebecca was in her kitchen in New Jersey, watching *Cooking with Chef Larsen* on a small TV. Larsen, known for his hair-trigger temper, had become the most popular chef on television. Right now he was berating a young chef for an undercooked calf's liver. He took the liver and made the chef wear it as a hat for the rest of the program. Rebecca's phone rang. She turned down the TV and looked at the caller ID. It was Jacob.

"Hi, Honey. How's Cleveland?"

"Is Beth there?" asked Jack, on the phone in his Massapequa garage.

"Don't be upset, but she went to Long Island to see Peter." As if on cue, Beth and Peter entered. Rebecca handed the phone to Beth. "It's your father, from Cleveland."

"Hello, Daddy," she said, flatly.

"Beth, please. I'm begging you, don't say anything to your mother."

"I'm sorry," she said. "Can't hear you." Beth handed Rebecca the phone, saying she lost the call.

"He'll call again," Rebecca said. "I am so happy to see you two back together. Peter, Beth knew you weren't like that."

"I'm not."

"Well, when you have time, you should see someone. That kind of hate doesn't come from nowhere. Beth, you should take him to the Holocaust Museum."

"Mom, there's something I have to tell you."

The phone rang again. Rebecca assumed it was Jacob calling back. Instead, it was her party planner, Richard, wanting to know if she had looked at the invitation samples. Rebecca and Jacob were having an anniversary party, where they planned to renew their wedding vows, in front of all their friends and family. "Twenty-five wonderful years," Rebecca said. "I only hope you two find as much happiness as we have."

Beth began to well up and ran out. "She's upset because we're not getting back together," said Peter, running out after her.

******

Peter and Beth sat on her bench at Hamilton Park. "I just didn't have the heart to tell her," said Beth.

"Been there," said Peter.

"And when she said she hoped we'd find the same happiness she has, it destroyed me."

There wasn't much more to say, but they were both thinking the same thing: *this is the last time we'll be together.* They sat in silence as darkness descended.

"I can't let you go," she whispered.

"You have to."

"Do you love me, Peter?"

"Stop it, my head's about to explode."

"We can do it."

"Do what?"

"Be together and love each other... just not in a certain way."

******

Rebecca sat at the kitchen table, looking at a sample invitation. Jack, wearing a Cleveland Indians jacket, came in through the garage door, carrying his suitcase. She wondered how he'd gotten home so quickly, since he just called from Cleveland a little while ago. He told her he had actually been calling from Newark Airport and forgot to mention it. She pecked him on the cheek and handed him the invitation. "What do you think?"

"You still want to have the anniversary party?" Jack asked, fishing.

"Why wouldn't I?"

"Beth hasn't said anything?"

"About what?"

"About the party. What does Beth think?"

"What does Beth think about what, Dad?" Jack turned and saw trouble — Beth and Peter, back from the park.

"Hello, Mr. Michaels," Peter said. "How was your auction in Cleveland? You must be a real fast talker to do what you do."

"Oh, he *is*," Beth agreed.

Jack wished he *was* in Cleveland. Getting Peter to join in the lie was hard enough, but Beth had always been headstrong and difficult to control, like when she had dropped out of Business College and entered that damn cooking school. She never listened to him. She was going to rat him out, and there was nothing he could do about it. "If you have something to say, say it," grumbled Jack.

"Peter and I are moving in together," Beth announced, defiantly.

"You're *what*?!" Jack shouted.

"We're in love," said Beth.

"That's wonderful!" said Rebecca.

"Yes, *isn't it, Daddy*?" said Beth. "Are you happy for us?"

"I thought he was a bigot," said Jack.

"Sometimes, people aren't what you think they are," said Peter.

"I don't care what you are, you're not living with your— her! It's a sin."

"Oh don't be so old fashioned, Jacob," said Rebecca. "We lived in sin for two years."

"You weren't my daughter!"

"Mother, Daddy and Peter obviously have some things to work out," Beth said. "Why don't we leave them alone?"

"Be nice to him, Jacob," Rebecca cautioned. "He could be your son-in-law."

"No, he can't!" snapped Jack.

Rebecca and Beth disappeared into the living room.

"Are you out of your *mind*?" Jack said. "You can't shack up with your sister. It's against the law."

"So's bigamy!"

"It's immoral."

"You're one to talk."

"Hey, I didn't sleep with my sister."

And it was true. Jack never even fantasized about his sister. And she walked around in her bra all the time. Luckily, she stopped talking to him thirty years ago, after an ugly dispute over their father's will concerning his baseball card collection, so it meant one less person he needed to lie to. Speaking of lying, there was a repeat performance in front of Peg. Just like Rebecca, she was thrilled the kids were back together, and happy that Peter was finally moving on with his life. Jack, of course, had to act surprised, but he wasn't pleased that Peter and this *Jewish girl* were about to live in sin.

THE ARRANGEMENT

SIN WAS A SIX FLOOR WALK-UP BROWNSTONE on a tree-lined street in Astoria, Queens. Below the stoop was a basement apartment with a sign in the window that said: "Florence Odetts - Psychic Readings." Parked in front of the building was a U-Haul truck. Peter pulled the strap at the bottom of the rear door and it slid up. He and Beth started unloading moving boxes. Peter took a box from the truck, turned and saw Jack standing there. He grabbed the box from his son and put it back on the truck. "I'm not letting you go through with this insanity." Jack reached up, grabbed the strap and pulled the sliding door down on his other hand, screaming in pain.

Upstairs, in apartment 5B, a small, furnished one-bedroom, Beth was sitting at the kitchen table, bandaging her father's hand. "It's my gavel hand," complained Jack.

"It should have been your head," Beth said. She felt

like stabbing him with the scissors she held, but instead she used it to cut the gauze.

"Why are you doing this to me?" whined Jack.

"*You*?" said Peter.

"It's the only way we can be with each other," explained Beth.

"But, it's sick."

"We're living together, not sleeping together. Right, Peter?"

"That's the plan."

Peter had read Plato's *Symposium* and understood the concept of how physical attraction is for the purpose of material pleasure and procreation, and how platonic love transcends into spirituality. He understood it, but he never thought he'd actually have to consider doing it.

"And how long do you think that's gonna work?" asked Jack.

Good question, thought Peter.

"Forever," Beth said. "There's more to a relationship than just sex."

"But you're attracted to her," Jack said to Peter. "How do you just erase that?"

Another good question.

"With restraint, Dad," Beth said. "Something you know zero about."

"I give it a week." Jack stormed out, slamming the door behind him.

"Can you believe him judging us?" said Beth.

"He's a megalomaniacal narcissist," added Peter.

"He's an *asshole*."

******

Peter and Beth's blatant disregard for his feelings pissed Jack off so much, he drove straight to Dr. Salvatore's office.

"So they're living together, platonically," said the therapist.

"How is that possible?" Jack asked.

"Don't underestimate the power of spiritual love."

"So you condone what they're doing?"

"I don't make judgments, Jack. If I did, I wouldn't be here with you."

"Hey, I'm not that bad a guy. I took Todd into my family, didn't I?"

"Yes, you did, but I often wonder, why?"

Jack remembered the day he first met Todd. He had slipped into the men's room at the Jewish Center to take a call from Peg, who thought he was in Tulsa at a livestock auction. Jack told her he loved her, and would be back home in Massapequa in time to go to church on Sunday, and would play with Peter that afternoon in the father/son golf tournament. Wanting to end the conversation, he made a loud mooing sound, telling her the first cow had arrived at the viewing stand and it was time to start the bidding. He clicked off, then heard a flush from the handicapped stall. Jack had thought he was alone, but the door opened and a twelve-year-old boy in a wheelchair rolled out.

"Hello, Mr. Michaels. Remember me? I'm the foster kid Rabbi Feldman told you about. The one you didn't want."

"How much did you hear, Todd?"

"Ohhhh, probably enough to make me a member of your fuckin' family. Going once... going twice..."

"Let's get back to my real kids," Jack said to Salvatore.

Jack wanted Dr. Salvatore to help him figure out a way to bust up Peter and Beth without antagonizing them, so they wouldn't squeal on him. The therapist pointed out his job was to help Jack deal with his emotions, not help him do his dirty work. Jack offered him an extra fifty for the session if he'd reconsider.

******

Peter and Beth spent the rest of the day unpacking and setting up their apartment like any other young couple, with one caveat; Peter was to sleep on the futon while Beth slept in the bedroom. The place was sparsely furnished, except for the kitchen, which Beth had stocked with everything necessary to prepare gourmet meals. Peter was finishing one of those meals, Sole Amandine, at the kitchen table while

Beth was busy at the stove, stirring something.

"When your mom is cooking, does he like to sneak up from behind and nibble on her ear?" Peter asked.

"I used to think it was cute. Now it turns my stomach," Beth said. "Here, taste."

She popped a spoon in his mouth.

"Awesome. What is it?"

"It's Chef Jean Claude's secret Panna Cotta recipe. He shared it with me 'cause I'm teacher's pet."

"I hate when my students suck up to me."

"I don't suck up," Beth said. "I'm just good at what I do."

Especially in those jeans, thought Peter. *Stop! This is my sister.*

"You know, one of the perks of living with a culinary student is you can expect gourmet dinners every night," Beth said.

"Every night?" Peter asked, licking the spoon clean.

"Every night, except Fridays and Saturdays. Beth explained that on Fridays there's a sit-down dinner after school where the culinary students eat what they've prepared that day. She invited Peter to tomorrow's dinner, so he could meet some of her fellow students and her mentor, the great Chef Jean Claude. They'd be preparing lobster, six different ways.

"Lobster, huh? I guess it would be *shellfish* of me not to come."

"Please, no food jokes in front of Chef Jean Claude."

"Why? Won't he *lettuce*?"

"Maybe we shouldn't live together?"

"Okay, okay, I'm done. So what's up on Saturdays?"

"On Saturdays I thought we'd go out."

"Go out? Where?"

"You know, dinner, a movie."

"Like on a date?"

"Yeah, we can call it that. Saturday night's our date night."

"When we go on this date, what are the rules?"

"What do you mean?"

"Like, can we share dessert?"

"Of course."

"And at the movies, I don't suppose I can put my arm around you?"

"Not a good idea."

"What if you're choking on popcorn and I have to give you the Heimlich?"

"Let me choke."

"Beth, do you really think we can make this work?"

"Absolutely. We'll be like any other two people in love, minus the… you know."

******

BETH, IN GYM SHORTS AND A TEE SHIRT, was in the bathroom brushing her hair. Peter, in pajamas, sat on the futon couch and could see her through the open door.

"This is better than not being together, isn't it?" she said.

"Yeah, it is," he said, trying not to look at her.

"And you're sure you're okay on the futon?"

"I'm fine."

In fact, he wasn't. Have you ever tried to sleep on one of those things? As Peter tried to get comfortable, all he could think about was Beth in those gym shorts. To distract himself, Peter thought of his Grandma Lucy on her death bed, which was probably a lot more comfortable than the futon.

GOODNIGHT... SIS

It was Friday at the Culinary Academy, where Chef Jean Claude dropped a live lobster into boiling water. Jean Claude explained to his chefs-in-training that the lobster feels no pain. Each student had a lobster and a choice. Either boil him to death or split his head open. He then invited Beth to come up and show how it's done. Beth, always eager to impress Chef Jean Claude, took a lobster and drove a huge knife through its head.

"*Ouch!*" In the teachers lounge at Massapequa High, Lenny watched Peter gingerly bend down to reach the bottom shelf of the refrigerator.

"Lenny, would you get that yogurt for me?" asked Peter.

"What's wrong?

"Futon."

Lenny handed him the yogurt. "You just moved in with your girlfriend, and you're already on the futon?"

"She has the flu, okay?"

"My girlfriend had bronchitis. Didn't stop me. Every time she coughed, her whole body spasmed. I came like an elephant."

"There are other elements to a relationship besides sex."

"Name one."

******

Chefs Jean Claude, Wong and their students sat at a long wooden table, platters of various lobster dishes in front of them, including Lobster Newberg, Lobster Thermidor, Lobster Fra Diablo, Lobster Bisque, and even a Lobster Pot Pie. "Can anyone name a good wine pairing with lobster?" asked Chef Wong."

"Chardonnay," Peter answered, having just walked into the room.

"Who are you?" Jean Claude asked.

"Chef Jean Claude, everybody, I'd like you to meet Peter my… boyfriend," Beth said.

"Lucky you, Peter," the chef said. "Please join us."

Peter sat down between Chef Jean Claude and Beth. He was in obvious pain.

"Back?" Jean Claude asked.

"Futon," Peter answered.

"Tonight, take my bed," Beth whispered, a little too loudly.

"Don't you two sleep together?" Jean Claude asked.

"Of course we do," Peter said. "She had the flu last night."

"And she came to class?!" Jean Claude shouted. "Everybody spit out your lobster!"

On the drive home, Beth was extremely upset. "I had a good relationship with Chef Jean Claude, and now he thinks I'm unsanitary."

"'Lucky you?' What the hell does that mean?" said Peter. "And what business is it of his, where we sleep?"

"Chef has an incredible curiosity. It's what makes his dishes so fascinating."

"You find that guy fascinating?"

"I said his dishes are fascinating."

"And how come you wear those tight jeans to school?"

"It helps me get a better grade. Okay? But if it makes you feel any better, he has as much chance of getting into them as you do." As soon as the words were out of her mouth, she wished she had them back. They spent the rest of the ride in silence.

When they arrived back at their building, Peter told Beth to go up without him. He wanted to walk a bit. It was the first time since choosing to be together that he and Beth had been anywhere as a couple and it had resulted in a fight. This was not going to be easy.

Later that evening, Peter sat in pajamas on the futon. Beth, in her robe, entered from her bedroom. "Are we okay?" she asked.

"We're good. I'm sorry, I got a little jealous."

"You have no reason to be."

"It'd be different if... you know."

"I know. Well... good night, Peter," She walked into her bedroom and closed the door.

"Good night… Sis," he whispered.

THE PROPHECY

Peter's Saturday morning began with two perfectly poached eggs and a couple of extra-strength Advils. After breakfast, he and Beth headed out to explore their new surroundings, and were ecstatic upon discovering that their neighborhood was a veritable melting pot of ethnic cuisines and specialty shops. There was an Italian bakery with incredible canolis, and an Indian spice store where Beth picked up ingredients for Chana Masala, a dish made with chickpeas. They found a Vietnamese vegetable stand, a hand-made soap shop, a sushi bar, a used book store, where Peter found an old copy of *The History of the Decline and Fall of the Roman Empire*, a pawn shop, a head shop, a storefront church, a self-service yogurt place, and a Puerto Rican bodega. It was way different than living on a golf course.

"How lucky are we to live in this neighborhood?" said Beth.

"I'd say we're fortunate, I'm not so sure the term 'lucky' applies to us."

"Peter, stop it. We're lucky to have each other. And all these wonderful shops."

"I didn't see a drug store."

"Is your back still bothering you?"

"A little."

"Maybe you should go to that acupuncturist we passed."

"Sorry, I'm not about to become a human pincushion."

As they approached their building, arms full of groceries and goodies, they found an elderly woman, with long, flowing gray hair, giant hoop earrings, and a dress made of colorful silk scarves, sitting on the stoop. "Welcome to the building. I'm Mrs. Odetts."

"The psychic from downstairs," said Peter.

"Nice to meet you," said Beth. "I'm—"

"Beth, and he's Peter," interrupted Odetts.

"Oh my God! How did you know that?"

"Your names are on the mailbox. By the way, Peter, there's a pharmacy two blocks down."

"Mrs. Odetts, you are unbelievable," said Beth.

"You ain't seen nothin' yet. I always give new tenants a free reading. What do you say, kids?"

Peter, not one to believe in the occult, politely begged off, but Beth was curious. She handed him her shopping bags and entered Mrs. Odetts' apartment.

Peter headed upsairs.

Florence Odetts first became aware she was "special" at the age of seven, when, knowing nothing about football, she predicted the Chicago Bears would beat the Washington Redskins 73-0 in the 1940 NFL Championship game. When word spread of the little girl's psychic prowess, every big time gambler in New York came to see her, bearing gifts. Lucky Luciano gave her a Schwinn, but angrily took the bicycle back when she prophesized that in 1946 he'd be deported back to Italy. She was right.

Mrs. Odetts took Beth into a darkened parlor, lit only by a few flickering candles, the outside light obscured by velvet drapes covering the windows. In the center of the room was a small table set for afternoon tea.

"Is that incense I smell?" asked Beth.

"No, cannabis. Have a seat."

A stuffed cat stared at Beth from its perch on the window sill. This was Oscar, Mrs. Odetts' cat from the early '70s. The medium explained that Oscar met his demise when a young teenage boy named David Berkowitz, on orders from his neighbor's dog, took the cat up to the roof and threw him off. The irony was that the dog and Oscar were friends. They used to play together, all the time.

Odetts said Oscar was telling her Beth needed some tea. She poured her a cup, explaining that the leaves were soothing to the soul, then took Beth's hand and studied her palm. The lines revealed Beth would have great success as a chef — success beyond her wildest dreams. Then, a concerned look appeared on the old woman's craggy face. She told Beth she saw that she and Peter were deeply in love, but their future together is uncertain. A man is standing in the way.

"Is it my father?" Beth asked.

"I can't see his face. I do see a boy in a wheelchair at a wedding… your wedding."

Beth was crestfallen. *If there's a wedding, the groom can't be Peter.*

Upstairs, in the apartment, Peter was putting away the groceries they bought, and thinking about the day. In the daytime, things are fine. He couldn't have had a better time exploring the neighborhood with Beth. They were just like any other couple. But, at night, when they're alone in this apartment, everything changes.

A few minutes later, Beth walked in, and Peter asked how the reading went. Beth told him Mrs. Odetts said she and Peter were deeply in love and would be together forever. Then, she quickly changed the subject, suggesting they go online and pick a movie for their date that night. The choice was not that easy. Peter thought they should avoid anything romantic. It might make them both uncomfortable. She hated action/adventure, and he hated horror, so the only thing left was the latest Smurfs movie, which Peter had already seen. They agreed to forego the movie and try Koji's, the sushi restaurant down the street.

Beth couldn't stop thinking about the old woman's prophecy, as a light snow began to fall on the way to the restaurant. Despite what Mrs. Odetts had predicted, Beth tried to remain steadfast in her belief that she and Peter could overcome the formidable odds against them. By the time they got to Koji's, Beth had convinced herself that the fortune teller was as phony as her story about Son of Sam killing her cat.

At the restaurant, they were warmly greeted by Koji, the owner, who had a way about him that made them feel like regulars. He recommended they sit at the sushi bar where he would be their chef. Beth was thrilled to sit at the bar and watch a master sushi chef in action. She told Koji she was a culinary student and part of her training included learning to make sushi. Koji invited her to come behind the bar and show him her stuff. Beth was nervous, but, with Peter's encouragement, she joined the chef, and, under his watchful eye, made an excellent California roll. The chef, Peter, and the couple sitting next to him applauded. Beth did a little bow, then came around and joined them at the bar.

The couple, Chrissie and Rick, had just moved into the neighborhood a few weeks before, coincidentally in the same building, in apartment 6B, right above Peter and Beth. Koji's was already their favorite restaurant. Rick warned them about the Mexican place down the street. Chrissie found a toenail in her tamale. Koji told them that in some countries, toenails are a delicacy. They all laughed, but he was dead serious. This was going really well; a local restaurant Peter and Beth could call their own, and a couple they could be friends with.

Rick, a New York City cop and Chrissie, a nurse in the children's ward at Mount Sinai, told Peter and Beth they'd been dating for a year and had just decided to move in together. Their plan was to get married and have lots of kids.

The same thought hit Peter and Beth simultaneously. *These two are living the life that we can never have.* "We don't believe in marriage or kids," Peter said. "We just like living together."

"Don't you find living together makes having sex a lot easier?" Chrissie asked.

Peter and Beth looked at each other. This was becoming painful.

"Frankly, we've been so busy unpacking and putting our place together…" said Beth.

"We've hardly had time," interjected Peter.

"We went at it as soon as the movers left," Rick said. "Chrissie is insatiable."

"So, if you hear screaming late at night," Chrissie said, somewhat embarrassed, "it's moi."

Peter had just met these two, and he already hated them. "Sometimes, a woman fakes screaming when she's not really being satisfied," Peter said. "Face it, Rick, you're not that attractive."

"Let's see how attractive you are after I put my fist through your face," fumed Rick.

"Let's just leave, Honey," Chrissie said. "We don't need Internal Affairs in our lives again." Rick and Chrissie made a quick exit. Peter downed the rest of his saké.

Beth touched his hand. "I'm sorry."

"This is hard, Beth."

On the walk back to their building, Peter was still upset about the incident at Koji's; not with Rick and Chrissie, but with his own overreaction. They were just making friendly conversation. If he and Beth were in a conventional relationship, they'd probably find Chrissie and Rick amusing. Beth agreed. She and Peter would have to learn to not be so sensitive when they socialized with other couples. When they got to their apartment, Peter decided to go upstairs and tell Rick he's sorry. "If I'm not back in twenty minutes, call Internal Affairs."

Peter knocked on apartment 6B. Rick answered, wearing only boxer shorts and a tee shirt. "You really think I'm unattractive?" he asked, a hurt look in his eyes.

"I think you're very attractive," said Peter, who went on to apologize for his behavior at Koji's.

"I think you're attractive, too," said the cop. "Would you like to come in and do Chrissie while I watch?"

"Gee, Rick. That's very neighborly of you, but I'm

gonna have to take a pass."

New York's Finest, thought Peter, as he went back down to the fifth floor.

When Peter walked into the apartment, Beth came out of the bathroom, fresh from a shower, wearing a pink terry cloth robe with a towel wrapped around her hair. As she commented on how fabulous the water pressure was, especially for a very old building, Peter could only think about how beautiful she looked and how good she smelled. Snapping out of it, he assured her everything was copasetic with the cop and the nymphomaniac. "We can go to sleep knowing that, once again, there is peace in the building." Peter downed a couple extra-strength Advils and said goodnight.

"Sure you don't want me to take the futon?" Beth asked.

"So you can kill *your* back? Go to bed. I'll be fine."

Two hours later, Beth, wearing her pink robe, entered from the bedroom and noticed Peter awake, tossing and turning on the futon. "That's it, we're sharing the bedroom," ordered Beth.

"You mean, sleep in the same bed?"

"Yes, sleep. It's a king. There'll be six feet between us."

Peter entered the bedroom and Beth closed the door.

"You really think this a good idea?" Peter asked.

"Don't worry, I'm not wearing my skimpy shorts and tight tee shirt."

"Good."

"I'm wearing *this*." She dropped her robe to the floor. She was naked! Peter screamed and ran for the door, but the doorknob came off in his hand. "Stop being such a baby, "Beth laughed. "There's a tribe in New Guinea that does this all the time."

Suddenly the bedroom door flew open. Standing there was Chef Jean Claude. "If you won't do her, I will," said the chef as he closed the door.

Peter bolted up on the futon. The bedroom door opened and Beth came out, wearing her robe. "Don't! We're not from New Guinea!" screamed Peter.

"No. You're from Long Island, and I'm from New Jersey, and you've been dreaming."

The nightmare shook Peter up. They had planned to go to the local farmers' market together the next day, followed by an art show at an Astoria gallery. But Peter begged off, saying he'd forgotten he had stacks of papers to correct for school on Monday, as well as fifty questions to make up for an exam on the Industrial Revolution. So, Beth went off alone, and Peter stayed in the apartment. There were no papers to mark, or questions to come up with. And no answer for Peter's dilemma.

LEAVE THE BOTTLE

Lenny sat in the bleachers of the Massapequa High School gym, reading *The Racing Form*, while his basketball team ran a fast break drill.

"Move it, Paparelli, you twink!" yelled Lenny. "That's why we lost to Hempstead."

"You forfeited that game, Coach," said one of the other players.

"What are you, Garcia, his lawyer?" Lenny said.

Peter walked into the gym, looking distraught. "I have to talk to you."

"Wanna go for a drink?"

"You're in the middle of practice."

"They are. I'm not."

******

At the Jean Claude Culinary Academy, the students were making gnocchi. Chef Wong told the group Chef Jean Claude would be arriving soon, with a special announcement.

"If I tell you something, you promise you'll keep it secret?" whispered Phil. "Me and Chef Wong."

"What about your golf pro, Tommy?" asked Beth.

"O-ver. I caught him kissing the Callaway salesman."

"Phil, I'm so sorry."

"Don't be, Chef Wong is an incredible lover. And Peter?"

"What about Peter?"

"How's his wong?"

"You know, there's more to a relationship than just sex." This was becoming her mantra. "There are moments between the two of you that are yours and no one else's."

"Tommy used to make a giant bowl of popcorn," Phil said, wistfully. "Then, we'd snuggle on the couch and watch *Dancing with the Stars* while he choked me. Is that what you mean?"

******

PETER AND LENNY WERE AT LUPE'S SOMBRERO. It was Lenny's favorite watering hole because teachers got a discount on tequila shots during school hours. Lenny ordered a couple of Cuervo Golds for himself and another one for Peter.

"Okay, what's so important you had to drag me away from practice?"

"You can't tell anybody," cautioned Peter.

"Sounds bad."

"Swear to me."

"On my mother."

"What would you do if you found out your girlfriend was your sister?"

"Have I fucked her yet?"

Maybe this was a mistake.

✶✶✶✶✶✶

TV's Chef Larsen was in his kitchen, talking to camera. "Today, we're making a beef stew recipe that's been in the Larsen family for over a hundred years. We'll start by cutting four pounds of chuck into one inch cubes." The camera zoomed in on the steak.

"Hey, what's with the close up of the food? I'm the star of the show, not some fucking piece of meat!"

"Cut!" Larsen's producer shouted."

"*Cut*?!" Larsen screamed. "I'll cut *you*, you *prick*." Chef Larsen ran toward the camera, brandishing a huge knife.

Chef Jean Claude and his students had been watching a recording of this incident on a TV monitor in the Culinary Academy. He turned off the video. The rest was too gruesome to watch.

"Unfortunately, my close friend Chef Larsen has been charged with attempted murder," said the chef. "But, there's good news. I've been asked to take over the show, and one of you lucky students will get to be my assistant — whoever makes the best gnocchi. You have twenty minutes."

"I'd blow him to get on that show," whispered Phil.

"I'm going with my gnocchi," said Beth.

******

Back at Lupe's, Peter had finished telling Lenny the whole sordid story. "So, your old man's been banging two wives for twenty-five years," Lenny said. "Sweet."

"*Sweet*?" Peter asked.

"I know you're close to this, 'cause he's your father, but if you step back for a second, you've gotta give Pops props for pulling this off."

"What he's done to me, and my sister, and our two mothers, is unconscionable."

"Tell me something, don't you think it's a little odd, living with your sister?"

"It's the only way we can be together."

"And when she parades around the house in her little thong panties, it doesn't affect you?"

"She doesn't parade around in little thong panties. She parades around in tiny little shorts, and tight little tee shirt."

"Whose brilliant idea was this anyway, yours, or hers?"

"Hers."

"Of course. No guy would come up with such crap. Listen, my pent up friend, people who are in love and *have* sex can't stay together. How are you two gonna do it?"

"I don't know."

"Lupe, give him another shot of Cuervo."

"And leave the bottle," said Peter.

******

Wasted, Peter trudged up the stoop to his apartment building and fumbled for his keys to the outside door.

"Other pocket."

Peter turned and saw Mrs. Odetts standing below, in front of her Psychic Reading Shop. Peter reached into his other pocket and found his keys. "Thanks," he said, unlocking the door.

"Remember," said the old woman. "It's not what you think it is, unless it is. Keep in touch." Peter regarded her curiously, then entered the building and stumbled up the stairs.

When Peter opened the door to his apartment, he saw Beth and Chef Jean Claude close together at the stove. She was wearing her tight jeans.

"Peter, you're home," said Beth.

"Yeah, I live here," Peter barked.

"You've been drinking tequila, haven't you?" said Jean Claude.

"How do you know?"

"Chef uses a lot of booze in his cooking," explained Beth.

"I don't mean to be rude, Chef, but why are you here?" asked Peter.

"I'm showing her how to make rice. Is there a problem?"

"She knows how to make rice. *I* know how to make rice."

"This isn't just any rice. This rice will be seen by millions," boasted Jean Claude.

"Chef is taking over the *Cooking with Larsen* show, and I'm going to be his sous chef," Beth said. "How awesome is that?"

"How'd *you* get the job?" Peter snarled.

"He loves my gnocchi."

"I bet he does."

"I think I should go," said Jean Claude.

"I think you should go, too," agreed Peter.

"Beth, I'll see you tomorrow," said Jean Claude, as he hurried out.

"What was that about?" asked Beth.

"I walk into my apartment and my... woman or whatever it is I'm supposed to call you, is pressed up against some dude."

"That 'dude' is my teacher."

"Well, what is he doing in our apartment?"

"Would you rather I had gone to *his* apartment?"

"Why couldn't you use the cooking school?"

"They're spraying for rats at the school."

"Guess what? I smell one."

"Peter, we were just preparing for tomorrow's show."

"Well, I don't approve."

"Approve of what?"

"Of you and him together, on the pretense of rehearsing for some cooking show."

"'Pretense?'"

"That's right, 'pretense.' If it walks like a duck and it quacks like a duck, it's a *duck*... especially if it's wearing 'fuck me' jeans."

"These are not 'fuck me' jeans. They're 'get a better grade' jeans." Beth went to the stove and stirred the rice. "I can't believe you think I would be with somebody else."

"Sorry if I'm a little insecure."

"You have no reason to feel insecure," she said, turning to him.

"Lenny thinks I do."

"You told *Lenny* about us?"

"I needed someone to talk to."

"Why didn't you talk to *me*?

"Because he's a guy, and I'm a guy, and you're not a

guy, which is the problem."

"So this is about sex."

"It's about intimacy and closeness, too. Everything a real couple has."

"We *are* a real couple."

"Real couples can put their arms around each other in the movies."

Peter took her face in his hands. He was never more in love with her than he was at that moment. "Don't you see, Beth? This is impossible."

✶✶✶✶✶✶

MRS. ODETTS TOOK A LONG HIT from her bong, peeked out her front window and saw a grim Peter emerge from the building, carrying his duffle. She had seen this storm coming, and felt sorry for the young couple, but was powerless to intervene.

Peter wandered the streets, lost in thought. *I just broke up with my sister. This is so sick it's almost funny.* Everywhere he went, he saw couples in love, like the young hipsters making out on the corner, or the seniors at the bus stop holding hands. Even the two mounted police horses in front of the movie theater were nuzzling each other. Peter glanced up at the marquee: *KING KONG*.

As the ill-fated love story of the giant gorilla and the beautiful Ann Darrow unfolded, Peter felt as if he was watching his own story, minus the natives, the human sacrifices, and the giant dinosaurs. He fought back tears as Kong stood atop the Empire State Building, gently holding Ann in his huge hand while planes shot at him. Mortally wounded, he looked at her lovingly, carefully put her down, then plunged to his death, a hundred and two stories below. Peter thought to himself. *You never had a chance, big guy. And neither did I.*

MONICA LEWINSKI'S HAT

Lenny was alone in his apartment, texting his vote for *America's Got Talent,* when the doorbell rang. It was Peter, carrying his duffle.

"Told you so," said Lenny.

Peter put down his gear and looked around. In all the years he'd known Lenny, this was actually the first time he'd been in his apartment. There was an 80 inch flat screen TV and a collection of weird items, including a tuba, a phone booth, a cigar store Indian, a Civil War cannon, and a skeleton in a dentist chair wearing a beret. Lenny was an eBay junky. He took the beret off the skeleton and handed it to Peter. "Monica Lewinski's hat. Seventeen bucks. And the couch you're gonna sleep on, twelve." Then he walked out to the balcony. Peter put Monica's hat back on the skeleton and started unpacking. He wondered if Beth missed him as much as he was already missing her.

Lenny called out from the balcony, "Hey, come check this out."

Peter walked out on the balcony and saw Lenny looking through an enormous telescope.

"Here." Lenny stepped aside. "A little somethin' to take your mind off of your sister."

Peter looked through the eyepiece. "Jesus! She must be in her eighties!"

"So, she's not allowed to take a bubble bath?"

Lenny took another peek. "Come on, Grandma. Soap them puppies up."

"I'm gonna go unpack," said Peter.

The next morning, Peter was in a deep sleep on the couch, thanks to emotional exhaustion and the fact that he was no longer on the futon. A female voice woke him. He looked up at the giant TV and saw an attractive newscaster with the CNN logo on the bottom of the screen. The news was devastating. A seven-point-six earthquake had hit Guatemala, leaving thousands dead, most of them women and children. Peter glanced over and saw Lenny gawking at the newscaster with his hand inside his pajama bottoms, moving rapidly to and fro.

"Don't you have a TV in your bedroom?" Peter asked.

"Yeah, but it's not high-def. Go make us some breakfast. The weather girl's about to come on and I'd like some privacy."

Peter gladly hightailed it into the kitchen. The sink was piled high with dishes, and there were roaches on the window sill. He opened the refrigerator and was immediately hit by the stench of rotting food. There was a yogurt with green fuzz oozing out of it, a half eaten egg salad sandwich with teeth marks, a slimy cucumber, and a wedge of moldy green cheese.

"Peter! Quick, I need help!" yelled Lenny.

Peter shut the refrigerator and rushed out, finding Lenny in the bathroom with the door open, standing proudly by the toilet. "Tell me that's not a world's record." Peter looked in the bowl and dry heaved. Lenny handed Peter his cell phone. "Now where should I stand so you can get us both in the shot?"

WELCOME HOME

> *jacob and rebecca michaels*
> *request your presence*
> *at the somerset jewish center*
> *in celebration of*
> *twenty-five wonderful years of marriage*

JACK STARED AT THE INVITATION in wide-eyed disbelief. "Beth's parents are renewing their vows," Peg said. "Isn't that romantic?"

Jack threw the invitation on the kitchen table. "Why would they invite us? We've never even met these people."

"Yes, but their daughter may end up marrying our son."

"Will everybody quit saying that?"

"Who's 'everybody?'"

"It doesn't matter, because I'm going to be out of town."

"How do you know? It's three months away."

He took out his smartphone and pretended to look at the calendar. "Here it is: March 25th, Kansas City, Boat Auction."

"I really don't want to go without you."

"Then, don't. If Peter and that girl stay together — and I wouldn't bet on it — there'll be plenty of time to meet her parents."

"Why are you so down on the kids?"

"'Cause I can tell when two people don't belong together." The doorbell rang. "And trust me, these two people do not belong together."

Jack opened the door. Peter stood there with his duffle.

"See," said Jack, taking Peter's bag. "Welcome home, Son."

The last place Peter wanted to end up was back here with his father, but life with Lenny was too disgusting, and Peter was financially tapped out. He and Beth had signed a year's lease on the apartment in Queens, and since leaving was his decision, he felt an obligation to continue paying his half of the rent. Beth loved the neighborhood, and Peter would never have asked her to move back to New Jersey and do what he'd been forced to do, live with Satan.

The most difficult thing for Peter about living at home was putting up the façade, in front of his mother, that the relationship between him and his father was the same as it had been before he found out what a scumbag Jack was. That meant eating meals together, playing in the Father/Son Golf Tournament, and toasting the "perfect couple" at the Blue View Golf Club Couple of the Year dinner, honoring his parents.

"Mom. You have what no other woman has." *Except for the woman in Somerset, New Jersey*, he thought. "And Dad. What can I say about you that hasn't already been said?" *You miserable, cheating motherfucker!*

Peg had sensed some tension between Peter and Jack, like the time Peter "accidentally" spilled hot tomato soup on Jack's head, or when he drew devil ears on his father in the family photo. She attributed Peter's mood swings to his breakup with Beth — which wasn't entirely wrong.

MELISSA OF ALBUQUERQUE

"Now I understand why you were so secretive about your sex life," said Phil, as he blowtorched the surface of a Crème Brûlée. "There *was* none. You're lucky it happened now, because the relationship was doomed."

"How stupid was I?" said Beth.

"You weren't stupid, you were in love. Granted, it was your brother, but… Look, what you need to do is move on. There are plenty of fish in the sea you're not related to."

Beth forced a smile. She was a bit conflicted as to whether she should tell Phil. Now she was glad she did. Losing Peter was bad enough, but having to keep everything to herself made her twice as miserable. Phil reminded her she had a lot to look forward to. And she did. So, Beth threw herself into her schoolwork and her exciting new position as the chef's assistant on the *Cooking with Jean Claude* television show.

✶✶✶✶✶✶

"And now, America's favorite culinary couple... Chef Jean Claude and his favorite sous chef... Beth!"

Chef Jean Claude and Beth, wearing a chef's jacket and her "get a better grade" jeans, came out on the set and greeted the audience. Jean Claude put his arm around his attractive costar. "Today Beth is going to cook one of her favorite recipes."

"Butternut squash soup," added Beth.

"Why do you keep torturing yourself?" asked Lenny. Peter was watching the program on the TV in the teachers' lounge at Massapequa High. "You've been watching this show everyday for three months."

Beth continued her demonstration on the TV. "I've already cut my squash into one inch chunks and melted the butter in a large pot. Now let's add chopped onion and cook it until it's translucent."

"While that's cooking, we have a tweet from Melissa Lopez of Albuquerque." said Jean Claude. *"Chef Jean Claude, you and Beth have such chemistry on the show. My question is: Are you sleeping together?"*

"Melissa, let's just concentrate on the squash," said Beth.

"Answer my question!" yelled Peter at the TV.

"You're Melissa?" asked Lenny.

"Of Albuquerque," said Peter.

"Dude, I know you're envisioning your sister sitting on Cheffie's face, but you've got to get that picture out of your mind."

"It wasn't in my mind, 'til now."

Lenny grabbed the remote and started changing the channels until he landed on *MTV's Spring Break*, Panama City, Florida, where a line of hot, bikini-clad coeds were on the beach stage, showing off their bodies.

"Ohhhhh. Look at *that*," said Lenny.

"Put back my cooking show," said Peter.

"Spring break, now there's something we've never done. Easter Vacation's coming up."

"I'm not going to Florida."

"Come on. Look at them."

The girls were now bending over, shaking their tight little asses.

"Those are just a bunch of wild young girls who are there for only one reason, to drink and have sex," said Peter.

"Go on."

"I have responsibilities here."

"What responsibilities? Your life is in shambles."

The girls were now tongue-kissing one another for prizes.

"If we leave tomorrow, we can get there in time for the *Miss Camel Toe* contest."

"There's no such thing as a *Miss Camel Toe* contest."

"You'll never know, unless you go. Besides, you're about three days away from putting a rope around your neck and jumping off a chair."

Lenny was not far off. Peter could use a change of scenery, and some fun. What the hell, the worst that could happen is he'd come back with skin cancer — and then, he wouldn't have to use the rope and chair.

SID ROSENBERG AND HIS SEXTET

Beth sat with Chef Jean Claude, among friends and relatives in the synagogue of the Somerset Jewish Center. Jack, wearing a yarmulka and tallit, stood under a chuppah, opposite Rebecca, Rabbi Feldman standing between them.

"Behold, you are betrothed unto me with this ring," Jack said, placing a wedding ring on Rebecca's finger.

"According to the law of Moses and Israel, I now pronounce you husband and wife," said the Rabbi.

Jack stomped on a napkin-wrapped glass, smashing it.

"Mazel Tov!" said the Rabbi. As the guests applauded, the Rabbi whispered in Jack's ear, "I hope you choke on the kugel."

"Just stay away from my wife," snarled Jack.

"Which *one*?!" shouted the Rabbi, as Jack led Rebecca back up the aisle.

Soon after the ceremony, about a hundred guests

gathered in the Jewish Center ballroom to schmooze and nosh on hors d'oeuvres of smoked salmon, cauliflower kugel bites, and chopped liver mini-knishes, all compliments of the famous Chef Jean Claude. The band, New Jersey's own Sid Rosenburg and his Somerset Sextet, had also played at Jacob and Rebecca's wedding.

Sid stepped up to the microphone. "On this day, twenty-five years ago, Rebecca and Jacob danced to this Stevie Wonder classic. Now put your hands together as the loving couple does it again."

Chef Jean Claude, Beth, and her brother Todd watched as Rebecca and Jack came out on the floor to dance, as Sid sang, "I just called to say I love you." Beth thought to herself, *You mean, I just called to say I'm lying.*

"Having fun, Todd?" Jean Claude said, trying to score points with Beth's adopted little brother.

"I'm in a fucking wheelchair, Chef Boyardee, or haven't you noticed."

Jean Claude turned his attention to Beth. "Look at your parents. This must be a very special moment for you." It was a "moment," all right. Beth was dying inside, and seeing her parents so happy together was what was killing her. She wished she could go up there, grab the mic from Sid, and tell the world what a selfish bastard her father really was.

"Beth, come out here and dance with Dad," said Sid, over the PA system.

"Shit," muttered Beth, as she went to dance with her dad.

"Shit?" said Jean Claude.

"You know," said Todd. "Big, brown, sometimes has corn in it."

"Chef Jean Claude, don't leave Mom hanging," said the bandleader.

On the dance floor, Jack was trying to ingratiate himself with Beth. "I really appreciate you doing this for your mother."

"Tell me, Daddy," Beth asked. "Are you renewing your vows with Peter's mother, too?"

Meanwhile, Chef Jean Claude was trying to ingratiate himself with Beth's mother. "I'm crazy about your daughter, Mrs. Michaels."

"I read in *People* magazine you were married before," said Rebecca.

"I was. Unfortunately, Loretta loved my food as much as I loved her, which is why she ballooned to three hundred and forty pounds. I lost her, during gastric bypass surgery."

Jack and Beth danced by. "What can I do to make you not hate me?" pleaded Jack. "Do you want me to tell your mother the truth?"

"Yes," said Beth.

"I was speaking hypothetically."

"How about if I hypothetically stick a toothpick in your eye?"

"Now, *everyone*, come join our happy family," said the bandleader.

All the guests came out on the floor. Jack left Beth to dance with Rebecca and Jean Claude went over to dance with Beth.

"So, when you danced with your father, did you put your feet on his, like when you were a little girl?" asked Jean Claude.

"Take me home," said Beth.

MISS CAMEL TOE

AN ATTRACTIVE FEMALE BARTENDER in her mid-twenties served mojitos to Peter and Lenny as they sat at their hotel's beachside bar, near the MTV stage in Panama City. "You're right," Peter admitted. "A change of scenery is exactly what I needed. The Florida coastline is magnificent."

"What coastline?" said Lenny, transfixed on the stage where a line of girls were being hosed down for a wet t-shirt contest.

Peter, wearing a Mets cap, Nike t-shirt and bathing suit, was looking at the ocean. Lenny, in a "Jay-Z" tank top and board shorts, suddenly recognized one of the girls on the stage. Linda Romano, a hot sixteen-year-old he taught a few years ago, was now, "over eighteen and fair game."

Peter was appalled. "You're actually going to try to nail one of your former students?"

"Hey, at least she isn't my sister," Lenny said. "Sorry,

you had that coming."

Two young coeds in skin-tight bikinis sat down next to the guys and introduced themselves as Ashley and Taylor. The girls, both BYU students and devout Mormons, were waiting to compete in the *Miss Camel Toe* contest.

Lenny put his arm around Peter. "See, never doubt me when it comes to vagina." Lenny then introduced himself as Justin, and Peter as Vance, both seniors from NYU. Peter apologized for his friend and told them his name is really Peter, a history teacher at Massapequa High. Lenny explained to the girls that Vance sometimes has delusions from a head injury he suffered while they were searching for children in the rubble of the Guatemalan quake. "He not only forgets, who he is, but also that we're here to have *fun*."

"It's time to anoint *Miss Camel Toe*," announced a sleazy voice from a loudspeaker. Ashley and Taylor asked the guys if they wanted to come watch. Lenny happily took off with the girls, but Peter opted to stay and finish his drink, which he did about thirty seconds after Lenny left.

The bartender poured Peter another mojito, and said she couldn't help overhear his friend's bullshit. She'd heard a lot of lines, but rescuing children in the Guatemalan Quake was a new one. Peter told her Lenny is crude, but has a good heart. He's just been trying to get Peter out of the funk he's been in for the last couple of months.

"Your friend took you to the right place," said the bartender. "If there's any such thing as the anti-funk, it's Panama City at spring break."

Peter looked at the bartender. She was really quite beautiful.

"I'm Megan," she said, extending her hand.

"Vance," he said, taking it. She laughed, and poured him another drink.

Five mojitos later, Peter looked out at the beach, where thousands of spring breakers were bumping and grinding to the pulsating rap music playing over the MTV loudspeakers. In the crowd, he spotted Lenny gyrating madly with Ashley who was wearing a tiara and a *Miss Camel Toe* sash. He couldn't help but smile at that. Another hit of mojito, and Peter found himself starting to move to the beat. Before he knew it, he was out on the beach, bumping and grinding against Taylor. It's amazing what a little liquor, sun-kissed white sandy beaches, and thousands of smokin' hot college girls can do for depression.

So Peter and Lenny took in the entire spring break experience. The only trouble was, they did it in one day. The festivities continued with a spring break tradition on the deck of their beachside hotel, where scores of students were tanning their hard bodies and guzzling down drinks in party buckets and beer bongs. Peter and Taylor looked on as Lenny licked salt off the top of Ashley's breast, downed a shot of tequila, then took a slice of lime from her mouth. Next it was Peter's turn. He licked the salt off Taylor's breast. This *was* fun. Especially during the lime removal, when she spit out the lime and tongue-kissed him.

More drinks, and more "fun," as the guys water-skied, body surfed, slip & slided and parasailed over the Gulf of Mexico. They may have been wasted, but not too wasted to play beach volleyball against a couple of muscular jocks from USC, with the girls looking on. Lenny tapped a high one to Peter who tried to spike it, but got slammed to the ground. The girls rushed to him, cradled his head, and poured a drink down his throat.

******

"I NEED SOMETHING BIG, possibly with 3D and Internet capability," said Chef Jean Claude as he and Beth entered the electronics superstore around the corner from the cooking school. "I brought a DVD of our show, so we can see what we look like on all the TVs." As they approached the television section of the store, *MTV's Spring Break* was on all the sets, with thousands of college kids partying on the beach, while Pitbull performed on the stage. Jean Claude went to get a salesperson to put on his DVD. Beth continued to watch as the camera pushed into the crowd. Suddenly she saw Peter rubbing up against a hot college girl in a string bikini and a BYU t-shirt. Beth was heartbroken, but she realized Peter was doing the right thing by moving on, as she was, or at least was trying to do.

Although Jean Claude and Beth were billed as America's Favorite Culinary Couple, they hadn't actually been a couple until recently. He had been interested in her ever since she started cooking school, but, as far as Beth was concerned, their relationship was strictly professional. However, now things were different. She and Peter could never be together, and it was time she accepted that. Beth glanced at the TV and saw Peter on the screen again. Then, the picture changed to America's Favorite Culinary Couple.

******

IT WAS NIGHTTIME ON THE BEACH IN PANAMA CITY. Multitudes of partying spring breakers, including Lenny, Peter, Ashley and Taylor, were drinking, dancing and messing around, while hip-hop beats blasted from the throbbing sound system. Peter, totally tanked, pulled Ashley toward him. He was about to kiss her when he realized, she was Lenny! Suddenly Peter was lifted off the ground and passed around the crowd. He was spun around faster and faster above the throng, as everything swirled around him. Then, all went dark.

The darkness was pierced by excruciating bright light as Peter, hung over and sore, struggled to open his eyes, then squinted up at the sun. The beach was completely deserted, except for thousands of beer cans. As his vision cleared, he noticed Megan kneeling over him. "Looks like you had a little too much fun."

She took him back to the bar, put a cold compress on his head, and gave him a glass of tangerine juice with salt & vinegar chips to help cure his hangover, explaining that the salt and vinegar is supposed to create acetic acid, similar to the acid the stomach uses in processing alcohol. The Japanese have been using vinegar as a hangover antidote for centuries. Whoever came up with the "Hair of the Dog" theory had to be an alcoholic.

Peter was beginning to feel something he hadn't felt in a long time — attracted to someone other than his sister. *Thank God. Maybe this nightmare is finally over.* Megan had long, blond hair that cascaded like a waterfall down her back, crystal blue eyes, soft lips, and was really, really nice. She also made a hell of a mojito.

Megan thoroughly enjoyed being a bartender, especially at a beach resort where she met lots of interesting people, got to work outdoors, and made decent money. Sure, it got hectic during spring break, when the population increased by about 250,000 college maniacs, but it also meant lots of tips.

Born and raised in chilly Minneapolis, Megan came down for spring break when she was a junior at Augsburg College, and fell in love with the sunshine and the Panama City beach. She dropped out of school and never returned, landing a job as bartender at a local hotel, where she fell in love with Ricardo, the hotel activities director. The first eight months of their marriage was everything she dreamed it could be, until she found out Ricardo's "activities" included banging half the women in the Florida Panhandle. After that, she decided to put serious relationships on the back burner.

"Okay," Megan said. "I bared my soul. So, what's an intelligent guy like you, a schoolteacher, no less, doing at spring break with a bunch of wacked-out college kids?"

Peter hesitated. *What do I say? I'm down here because I'm trying to get over my sister?* The distress on Peter's face told Megan not to push it, so she took the pressure off. "Look, it's none of my business. I'm just a nosy bartender. Why don't you let me take you to dinner tonight?" Peter said it wasn't necessary, she'd done enough; but Megan insisted.

Megan brought Peter to a great little seafood place, far away from the drunken hordes, where they feasted on char-grilled grouper, fresh, plump Apalachicola oysters, jumbo Gulf shrimp stuffed with buttery blue crab, and spicy Cajun crawfish. By the end of the meal they were both so stuffed, they could hardly move. Megan suggested they walk it off on the way back to her house, which was on the way to Peter's hotel.

When they got to Megan's place, she told Peter she didn't have to be a mind reader to tell that he's down here trying to forget someone. "I know how hard it can be. If you ever want to talk, I'm here to listen, as a professional. That's what bartenders do." She squeezed his hand, gave him a quick kiss, then disappeared into her house.

On the walk back to his hotel, the memory of that little kiss lingered. For most of the night, until Megan brought it up, Peter was able to stop thinking about Beth and enjoy himself without getting hammered. As he neared his hotel, he could hear the throngs of spring breakers partying on the beach. He'd had it with that. But he was glad he had come down there because he had met Megan. He wondered if anything could happen between them. Megan was special. She was sexy, independent, and, best of all, she was not his sister. Maybe Lenny had been right to bring him down here. And, by the way, where *was* Lenny?

When Peter got back to their hotel room, Lenny wasn't there. Peter plopped down on his bed. He was feeling a lot better. Meeting Megan was an eye opening experience for him. He wondered how she'd react if he did tell her about Beth. Would she think he's some kind of freak? *He* couldn't even fathom what he and Beth had attempted. No, this secret would have to stay with Peter, Beth, their father, and Lenny.

Peter wondered what was on Megan's Facebook page, so he took out his smartphone, started to search for Megan on his homepage, and noticed a posting from Beth. He should have unfriended her months ago, but couldn't bring himself to do it, and, obviously, she hadn't unfriended him. It's hard breaking up in the age of social media. The post was a picture of Beth accepting a culinary award. She was wearing a spaghetti strapped gown and looked beautiful. He was about to hit the Like This icon when he stopped himself. *What am I doing?* He decided to take her off his Friends List. Next, he elected to stop following her on Twitter, to remove her from Friendster, Myspace, and Google +, strip her from Skype, drop her from Dropbox, then finally, and most drastically, to delete her from the "Contacts" list on his phone. But when he got to Beth's phone number, he couldn't do it. Instead, he thought about calling her, not for any purpose other than to congratulate her on the award, and that's it. Then he stopped, realizing he was just rationalizing. The healthy thing to do was delete the number and move on.

******

"BETH, THE WAY YOU SAUTÉED YOUR SNAPPER on today's show was delightful." Beth and Jean Claude were seated at a booth at Koji's. "You seem to be finally pulling out of your funk. Makes a big difference on camera."

"Thank you," Beth said. "I just had to accept the fact that Peter has moved on." *And is obviously having the time of his life without me.*

"A good chef needs to do that. Compartmentalize. The day after my wife's tragic death, I was back in the kitchen, making a fantastic *pot de crème*. You're going to be much better off with that history teacher out of your life."

He put his hand on hers. She knew the chef was right, but at the same time, the finality of losing Peter forever overwhelmed her with emotion. "Excuse me. I have to use the restroom." She got up, leaving her cell phone on the table. Koji came over with saké.

"Miss Beth break up with boyfriend?" Koji asked.

"Yes," Jean Claude answered.

"So you her boyfriend, now?"

"Not officially."

"Then why you touching her?"

"Just pour the saké, and mind your own business."

"You famous Chef Jean Claude, right?" Koji said, pouring the saké.

"Guilty."

"My grandfather die after eating in your restaurant."

"Mine died at Pearl Harbor. It's a push."

Koji walked off muttering to himself in Japanese. Beth's cell phone buzzed. Jean Claude looked at the name on the screen, and quickly answered it. "Peter?"

"Who is this?" asked Peter, calling from his spring break hotel room.

"Chef Jean Claude."

"Why are you answering Beth's phone?"

"She's in the bathroom. Do you want me to take a message, or should I get her?"

"Don't bother," said Peter. Then he hung up.

Beth returned from the restroom after regaining her composure. Realizing she might notice the caller ID on her phone, Jean Claude told her she had a call from Peter. "I took the liberty of answering, but it must have been a butt-dial. All I could hear were girls screaming and that horrible hip-hop music. Drink your saké."

Peter wished he hadn't made the call. He had just taken his pants off when the door opened and Lenny walked into the room with his former student, Linda Romano.

"Linda. You remember Mr. Michaels, the history teacher."

"Mr. Stokes said you needed a blowjob."

"Get her out of here!!!" screamed Peter.

Lenny gave Linda a pat on the butt and told her to wait for him in the bar.

"What's wrong?" said Lenny.

"I called Beth. Jean Claude answered her phone."

"That means he's fucking her."

"Do you have to verbalize every thought that comes into your head?"

"I didn't realize I said it out loud."

"I can't believe she's sleeping with that jerk."

Beth wasn't sleeping with that jerk. Not yet, anyway, but it wasn't for the lack of trying on the jerk's part. After their dinner at Koji's, and a few too many cups of saké, Jean Claude escorted Beth home, and, as he had done many times in the past, asked to come upstairs for a nightcap. Beth had always gently turned him down, but tonight, she found herself inviting him up.

In the apartment, they shared a bottle of Pinot Noir, and Beth was now officially lit. She looked at the chef. He was handsome enough, crazy about her, and he had made Beth a TV star. Where was the bad? As she sat close to Jean Claude on the futon couch, she found herself touching his leg with her hand. He put his arm around her and pulled her close. She closed her eyes as their lips met. When they broke apart, she took his hand and led him into the bedroom. This was something she needed.

THE PERFECT TONIC

WITH A LITTLE LESS THAN A WEEK LEFT before they were to return to Long Island, Peter and Lenny each made the most of the new relationships they had formed in Panama City. Lenny was actually starting to fall for Linda Romano. She was young, full of life, and had no gag reflex. Peter wasn't sure if he was falling for Megan, but he certainly enjoyed being with her.

When she wasn't tending bar, Megan spent as much time in or near the water as possible. Minnesota has its lakes, but nothing like the beauty of the Gulf of Mexico. She took Peter to a beach, far away from the maddening crowds. They walked barefoot on the soft, sugar-white sand, picking up seashells and colorful pieces of sea-washed glass. Megan looked amazing in her swimsuit. He'd never been a big fan of tats, but he found hers incredibly erotic, especially the butterfly tramp stamp disappearing into her bikini bottom.

I wonder if Beth has a tattoo someplace? Was there nothing that didn't start him thinking about Beth?

Megan suddenly stripped off her bathing suit, told Peter to take off his, and then ran off into the water. Well, his mind wasn't on Beth now! He took off his suit and joined Megan in the ocean. A minute later, they were in each others' arms. This was something he needed.

Peter spent the night in Megan's bed. And guess what? She was there, too. In the morning, when Peter woke up, Megan was already preparing breakfast for him: overcooked eggs, undercooked bacon, and burnt toast. Wonderful! This woman was nothing like "You-Know-Who." Couldn't boil an egg, but made a killer Bloody Mary. She didn't play golf, but she parasailed, snorkeled, and jet skied. And best of all, she wasn't his sister.

Megan was the perfect tonic for what Peter needed. They spent the rest of spring break having lots of sex and lots of fun. It would have been so easy to fall in love with Megan, but Peter wasn't ready, yet. Besides, spring break would be over soon, and he had to go back to the no-fun place, living with the father he detested. He and Megan promised to stay connected, by phone, Skype, email, Twitter, and, of course, text. School would be over in the middle of June, and Peter would be free to return to Panama City, if they were still feeling something for each other. No promises.

BAD SPINACH

Peter arrived home refreshed, rejuvenated, and recharged. He and Megan kept in touch and continued their long distance relationship. And, he was back to teaching, with the passion and the enthusiasm he had before. This week, he had the students erect a mock Berlin Wall in the middle of his classroom, and at the end of the week they got to knock it down. Like the East Germans who watched the real wall come down, he was actually feeling optimistic about the future.

******

"Any progress between you and Peter?" said Doctor Salvatore.

"We're talking," said Jack. "The other morning, he wished me bad luck on my colonoscopy."

"Well, that's some progress. And how's Beth doing?"

"She's moved in with that pompous chef," said Jack. "He's not half the man Peter is, but at least my grandchild won't have six heads."

******

"So what's it like, living with the great and powerful Jean Claude?" Phil asked, as he bit into a perfectly seared piece of Ahi Beth had prepared in the famous chef's apartment.

"He makes his toast one slice at a time, like anybody else," said Beth. Actually he didn't. Jean Claude had virtually created a restaurant kitchen in his SoHo apartment with a twelve-burner stove, walk in refrigerator, commercial oven, deep fryer and the latest in molecular gastronomy, including a Sous Vide machine, anti-griddle, and a liquid nitrogen device. There was even a tank with live lobsters.

"Girlfriend, when you move on, you move *on*," said Phil. Speaking of moving on, so had Phil. Or was it moving back? He had left Chef Wong and returned to Tommy, the golf pro. Phil said he realized that Tommy is, and always has been, the one. Chef Wong was just a temporary diversion. "It's so good being back with Tommy," said Phil. "He even choked me last night."

Beth was happy for Phil, but she'd accepted the fact that the same thing could never happen between her and Peter. And Beth was content here. She loved her old neighborhood in Astoria, but the Chef's SoHo loft wasn't a bad tradeoff. SoHo was loaded with restaurants, trendy boutiques, and art galleries. And there was nothing there to remind her of "You-Know-Who."

******

JACK STILL BELIEVED he could repair his relationship with his son, especially since Peter had given up the ridiculous idea of living with his sister, and was now involved with some bartender from Florida.

Peter was in the backyard, on Skype, talking to that very same bartender, who was dressed as Spiderwoman. There was a Comic-Con convention at the hotel. Megan was hit on by Thor, Iron Man, and Wolverine, but had resisted their super powers of seduction. She hadn't planned on it, but she missed Peter, a lot. Megan asked Peter who that man was, standing behind him. Peter turned around. It was Jack, waving at the screen.

"Megan, I'll Skype you later," said Peter. He shut the cover on his iPad.

Jack had gotten so used to Peter's hostility, it didn't even phase him anymore. He pulled out two tickets to the Mets game. "It's Dwight Gooden Bobble Head Night. You can put it right next to your Mookie Wilson."

"Go to Hell," muttered Peter.

"That's alright," Jack said. "Maybe my future

son-in-law, the chef, will go with me." Jack put the tickets into his pocket, grabbed his net and started fishing for golf balls. Peter shoved him into the pool.

✶✶✶✶✶✶

AS THE END OF THE SCHOOL YEAR APPROACHED, Peter began making plans to drive down to Florida, to be with Megan. He intended to stop on the way at Colonial Williamsburg, Fort Sumter, and Bunker Hill, historic landmarks he had always wanted to see. While in the process of booking a Williamsburg hotel during his free period, Peter got a text from Megan: *"HI."*

He texted back: *"HI."*

She texted: *"LOOK UP."* He did, and saw her smiling face in the back of his empty classroom.

He texted: *"WHAT R U DOING HERE?"*

She texted back: *"HAVING SEX WITH U, 2NIGHT?"*

He texted: *"I JUST GOT WOOD AND I'M NOT EVEN THE SHOP TEACHER,"* just as his fourth period class spilled into the room. Startled, Peter dropped his phone on the floor. One of his male students picked it up, looked at the screen, grinned, and handed it back to him. Now all eyes were on Megan, as she gave up her seat and sheepishly walked to Peter's desk. "I'll call you in a little while," she whispered, then started out, but he grabbed her arm.

"Everybody, I want you to meet my girlfriend, Megan."

The class hooted and howled their approval.

"Girlfriend?" Megan whispered. "I thought we were just fuck-buddies." She smiled and sashayed out, leaving Peter no choice but to sit down, because now, he really *had* wood.

******

Peter, exhausted and satisfied, watched Megan as she got out of bed and walked into the bathroom. Megan had accepted an offer from the hotel chain to bartend at their newly opened Midtown Manhattan location. At the end of the summer she could opt to stay in New York, or return to her regular gig in Panama City. She got a bump in pay and this beautiful hotel room, but best of all she got to be with Peter. Peter was disappointed he wasn't going to see Colonial Williamsburg, but seeing Megan naked was a close second.

Another bonus of spending time with Megan was less time at home with Daddy Two-Wives. Since school was over and Megan bartended at night, it gave them the opportunity to visit all the places Megan had only heard about, like the Guggenheim, MoMA, the Museum of Natural History, Coney Island, Ground Zero, the South Street Seaport, Rockefeller Center, and the Bronx Zoo.

On this night, Peter was taking Megan to Brooklyn's famous Peter Luger Restaurant, where the steak alone is reason enough to never go back to Panama City. Peter wanted to take the next step in their relationship, so he arranged with the waiter to have a promise ring hidden inside her apple strudel. He looked at Megan as she took a bite of her aged to perfection prime rib eye. She was absolutely beautiful, the best thing he could have hoped for. When the waiter saw Megan put down her fork, he wheeled over the dessert cart.

"I can't eat another bite," Megan said. "No dessert for me."

"You have to have the strudel," Peter said. "It's the reason everybody comes here."

"I thought it's for the steak."

"People in the know, know it's for the strudel," added the Waiter.

"Okay, okay. I'll have the strudel," said Beth.

"She'll have the strudel," smiled Peter.

"One strudel," said the waiter. He winked at Peter and wheeled the cart away to prepare the big surprise.

"I wonder what *they're* having for dessert?" Megan said.

"Who?"

"Have you ever seen that *Cooking with Jean Claude* show? Those chefs on the show — they're sitting over there."

Peter looked across the restaurant and saw Beth, in animated conversation with Jean Claude.

"I'm crazy about her," Megan said. "But he seems so full of himself. I don't know what she's doing with him."

Suddenly, all of Peter's repressed feelings came bubbling to the surface. His heart rate quadrupled and the room began to spin. "I'm not feeling that well," Peter said. "Tell him to put the strudel in a doggie bag. I've got to get some air." He handed Megan his wallet, took one last glance at Beth, and bolted out.

Peter steadied himself against a lamp post, trying to catch his breath. Seeing Beth, in the flesh, had brought on a full-blown panic attack. Thankfully, the cool night air was soothing, and by the time Megan came out from the restaurant, he had calmed down. He assured Megan he was okay. It must have been the creamed spinach.

On the subway ride back to Manhattan, Peter closed his eyes and reflected on what had happened. It was obvious he wasn't over Beth. But he *had* to be. Megan meant too much to him to lose over a woman he could never have. Peter opened his eyes and found Megan looking at him, lovingly. He put his arm around her. "How 'bout you try your strudel, now?"

"You were sick, and I'm still full," she said. "So I gave the strudel to that man over there."

Peter looked across the subway car and saw a happy homeless guy about to bite into the strudel. He dove across the car and snatched it out of his hand. Megan was horrified. "That's the most awful thing I've ever seen."

Peter fished out the ring from inside the strudel. "Is this awful?" He gave the homeless guy back the pastry, then handed Megan the ring. "I know we said, 'no promises'…" Megan was caught off guard. She'd wanted to keep her relationship with Peter fun and casual, having been hurt so badly in her marriage, but Peter was different. He felt "secure." She trusted him. Megan slipped the ring on, and put her head on his shoulder.

THE BOMBSHELL

"This Megan is the best thing that ever happened to me," said Jack.

"It would be nice if you were happy for Peter," said Dr. Salvatore.

"I'm happy for both of us. And, may I say, she is way hot. If I weren't happily married, and she wasn't my son's girlfriend… Anyway, Peter brought her home to meet us, and I charmed the pants off of her."

Jack raised his glass. "To my son, Peter, and the beautiful, intelligent, vivacious woman who has captured his heart… and mine." Peter had been apprehensive about bringing Megan home, but Peg insisted on meeting the girl who wore her son's promise ring.

Dinner was excruciating for Peter. He had had to listen to his mother prattle on about what a wonderful marriage she and Jack had, and how close the bond was between Peter and his father. Jack pointed out his number one priority has always been family, but the downside of being on the road so much was the time spent away from them. As much as Peter detested every lie coming out of his father's mouth, part of him marveled at the ease in which Jack came up with them. Could there actually be some truth to what he was saying? Did he really miss this family when he was over there, and vice versa? Peter snapped out of it. His father was a scumbag.

"So, what's your secret?" Megan asked Peg.

"Secret, about what?" Peg replied, a bit nervously.

"Filling your time, while your husband's away so much."

"Oh. Well, I golf. I read. I do Pilates. And, every Wednesday, I volunteer at the Cancer Club, I mean, Clinic." Peg poured herself another glass of wine.

"How lucky am I to have found this woman?" said Jack. "And you're lucky too, Peter. This one's a keeper. You should marry her before someone else does."

"Someone else did," said Megan, and went on to divulge the details of her failed marriage and the philandering ways of her ex-husband.

Jack chimed in with, "I wonder what compels some men to cheat?"

"Dancer's legs?" shot back Peter. Jack smiled. *Touché.*

"Dancer's legs, librarian's legs, flight attendant's legs… anything with legs," said Megan.

"According to CNN, just as many women cheat these days as men," said Jack.

"I saw that report," added Megan. "But most men cheat because it's sexually exciting, while women cheat because they're unhappy in their relationships."

"Can we stop all this talk about cheating?" pleaded Peg, reaching for her wine glass and knocking it over. Megan couldn't help but notice how inappropriately upset Peg was as she sopped up the mess with her napkin.

The rest of the evening was dominated by Jack's anecdotes about the interesting people he'd met along the auction trail. Megan seemed to be enthralled by Jack's stories, and Peter's mood grew worse and worse. It seemed like Jack *was* charming the pants off her. Always the salesman, he was best at selling himself.

On the drive back to the hotel, Megan apologized in advance for being so direct, but she wasn't buying any of Jack's bullshit. She did not believe for one moment that Peter and his father were close. She could sense the tension between them. And Peter's mother was a wreck. "Five glasses of wine at dinner? Forgive me, but this is not one big happy family."

Peter conceded Megan was spot on. He believed his father being away so much was the reason his mother drank. The tension between father and son wasn't so easy to explain. But Peter had strong feelings for Megan and he felt the need to be honest with her, so he delivered the bombshell.

"What my mother doesn't know is the reason he's away so much is because he's had a second wife and family in New Jersey for the past twenty-five years."

Megan was flabbergasted. "Why haven't you told her?"

Peter pulled over and shut off the engine. "I can't, it would destroy her. And there are other people involved."

"Like who?"

"Like Rebecca, his New Jersey wife. Todd, his handicapped, adopted son. And Beth, my half-sister."

"You know these people?!"

"Kinda. Beth and I dated for awhile."

"You dated your sister?!"

"When we first met, we didn't know we were brother and sister."

Peter told Megan the whole story, from the day he and Beth met on the golf course, to their breakup after having tried living together platonically. When Megan realized who Beth was, she knew Peter became ill at the restaurant because he saw Beth, not from bad creamed spinach.

"You're still in love with her, aren't you?"

Peter had no answer. He started the car and drove off.

At the hotel entrance, they sat in silence. Finally, he turned to her in desperation. "I just need time."

"No. You need lots of therapy." And with that, Megan walked into the hotel and out of his life.

GREG NORMAN

Peter was now back in his funk — big time. He didn't bother to shave or shower, and when he wasn't moping around the house, he was usually at Lupe's Sombrero, knocking down shots of tequila. There were angry outbursts, mixed with uncontrollable sobbing. He couldn't sleep, he couldn't eat, and he fell back to obsessively watching Beth's cooking show. In his insanity, he'd become quite the amateur chef. Peter had successfully learned to make shepherd's pie, linguini bolognaise, clams casino and a superb chocolate soufflé. Instead of eating the food he made, he smeared it on the walls in his room. His mother attributed this odd behavior to his breakup with Megan, but if it kept up much longer, he'd either have to see somebody or they'd have to repaint the room.

Peg was thinking about seeing somebody herself. Lately, her anxiety had been building, and she was well aware that her drinking had been getting out of hand.

Still in her nightgown, she was sitting at the kitchen table when the doorbell rang. It was Sandy. "Peg, why aren't you dressed? We're supposed to go to Bloomingdale's."

"I'm sorry, Sandy. I'm just not up to it."

"What's wrong, Sweetie?"

"Sandy, did you ever do something that made you despise yourself?"

"All the time. Then I go to Bloomingdale's to forget about it."

Usually, when Peg felt down, shopping *was* the tonic, especially at Bloomingdale's. So she went. She tried on earrings, hats, outerwear and underwear, but she couldn't find relief anywhere, not even from a pair of $625 Christian Louboutin pumps. She finally decided to hit the Men's Department and get a gift for Jack. Maybe it would alleviate some of the guilt she was feeling.

As she reached for a golf shirt, another woman did, too.

"I'm sorry. You were there first," said Peg.

"Thank you," said Rebecca. "My husband is a huge Greg Norman fan."

"Mine too," said Peg. "Do you play?"

"As much as I can. We live on a course."

"You're kidding? We do too." She extended her hand. "Peg Michaels."

That evening, in the New Jersey Michaels'

kitchen, Rebecca was at the stove cooking. Her husband sneaked up from behind and nibbled on her ear.

"You'll never guess what happened today, Jacob," said Rebecca. "I ran into Peter's mother in Bloomingdale's."

"*What*?!" The odds of both his wives running into each other were as astronomical as his son and daughter running into each other. He steadied himself, waiting to be busted.

"She invited us to join her and her husband, Jack, for a round of golf, tomorrow."

He heaved a sigh of relief. Obviously, the wives hadn't compared notes. Jack shifted into his prevent-defense.

"Why would we want to play golf with them? Our kids aren't together anymore."

"I know, but she and I hit it off."

"Ridiculous. You two are nothing alike."

"You don't even know the woman."

"Doesn't matter. I'll be out of town tomorrow, anyway. Tell them we'll play some other time." *Which means never*, thought Jack, confident he'd figure out how to keep these two women apart. After all, wasn't he the master of manipulation? At least, that's what Dr. Salvatore called him.

✶✶✶✶✶✶

Beth and Chef Jean Claude walked arm-and-arm, carrying groceries on the way to the Chef's SoHo loft. Peter crouched behind a parked car across the street and watched as they disappeared into the building. He took out a pair of binoculars and honed in on the chef's window. On the sill was a Dwight Gooden Bobblehead!

Peter sat down on the curb and thought back to when he was twelve, and his father took him to the Mets game for Mookie Wilson Bobblehead Night. There was heavy traffic on the Long Island Expressway, and by the time they arrived at Shea Stadium, all the bobbleheads had been given out. As luck would have it, the six-year-old in the seat next to Jack got hit in the head with a foul ball and had to be rushed to the hospital. In the commotion, the poor little fella left his bobblehead on the seat. Jack snatched it and gave it to Peter, telling him that's the way the world works. *Yeah, the world according to Jack.* Peter's thoughts were interrupted by a New York City policeman telling him to move along. Peter got up and handed the binoculars to the cop. "Do me a favor, Officer. Keep an eye on my sister."

Later, at the local precinct, Lenny came to bail Peter out. "Peeping Tom, that's gonna look swell on your teacher's resume." Peter didn't care about his resume or anything else.

The next day, Jack arrived at his Long Island home, suitcase in hand. He had told Peg he was at an estate auction in Bridgeport, Connecticut, when he was, of course, in Somerset with Rebecca. Now Rebecca thought he was in Bridgeport when he was in Massapequa. He was, in fact, going to be in Bridgeport tomorrow. Sometimes it got so complicated, even Jack had trouble following it.

A note on the kitchen table said, "2:00 PM tee time. Meet me on the practice range. Love Peg"

At the Blue View Golf Course practice range, Tommy McMillan, the golf pro, was holding a male pupil from behind, adjusting his swing. A few stalls away, Rebecca stood behind Peg as she hit a shot with her driver.

"I'm so glad you convinced me to come," Rebecca said, stepping up to the tee.

"I know what it's like to have a husband who's away a lot," Peg said. "Life shouldn't stop just because he's out of town."

Jack, in his golf cart, approached the driving range and screeched to a stop. *Holy shit! Both wives together!* He pulled his golf hat over his face and floored it, whizzing by them undetected. Jack drove the cart around the side of the clubhouse, safely out of their view as the starter announced, "Michaels threesome to the first tee."

"That's us," Peg said. "Jack will catch up when he gets here."

The women got into their golf cart and headed to the tee. When they arrived, Rebecca's cell phone rang. The caller ID read "Jacob." It was Jack calling from behind the clubhouse. "Don't panic, Honey, but I'm in Bridgeport General Hospital. They think it's a heart attack."

"Oh my God!" screamed Rebecca. She told Jack she loved him and would be there as soon as possible. Peg drove Rebecca to the club parking lot, where she jumped in her car and headed toward JFK, hoping to catch the next flight to Bridgeport.

Peg had just returned her cart when Jack pulled up in his, apologizing for being late. She anxiously told him all about Rebecca and her husband's heart attack. Jack put his arm around his wife. "Take it easy. I'm sure he'll be okay."

"I'm worried, Jack. When Rebecca told me her husband was having a heart attack it was like she was talking about you."

"Can I at least try out my new putter before I die?"

On the third hole, Jack purposely sliced his ball into the woods. He had Peg take the cart, saying he would meet her up on the green, then walked into the woods and took out his cell phone.

Rebecca was on the Southern State Parkway, headed toward JFK airport, when her phone rang. It was Jacob, calling from "Bridgeport General." False alarm, the heart attack turned out to be acute indigestion.

He was fine. Relieved, but still somewhat frazzled, she passed the airport and drove back toward New Jersey.

Jack emerged from the woods and headed for the green. He had just dodged the most dangerous bullet in all his years of bullet-dodging. There had been other close calls, but nothing close to this. Like the time he was a hostage in a Somerset, New Jersey Bank holdup with Peg thinking he was in South Carolina, auctioning off Civil War artifacts. As the police led the robbers and hostages out of the bank, in front of heavy media coverage, the robbers covered their faces... and so did Jack.

When Jack arrived at the green, Peg was on the phone. It was Rebecca, with good news. Her husband was okay. In reality, her husband wasn't okay. The close calls were getting closer and Jack felt vulnerable. If he didn't find a way to keep Peg and Rebecca apart, he was doomed.

Jack considered various plans. He could sell one of the houses and move far enough away so the wives would be too far apart to get together, but that would also make his drive between houses longer. Besides, he'd already paid for side-by-side cemetery plots in Long Island and New Jersey, for himself and each wife. He was never quite sure how that would work out, but he'd be dead, so it wouldn't matter. *That's it! Fake my own death. Only which one of me dies, Jack or Jacob?*

It would have to be Jack. No way am I giving Rabbi Feldman a shot at my widow. Jack knew the perfect spot on Oyster Bay where he could make it look like his corvette careened into the ocean and his body was swept away. *But what if Peg invites Rebecca to my memorial service and she sees the giant picture of me above the empty coffin. Then I'm really dead.*

"How do we stop these two women from getting together?"

"We?" said Dr. Salvatore.

"Okay, I."

"I don't think you can. These women are connected now. And you, my friend, are the connection. It's over, Jack." And, after two and a half decades of deception, Jack was faced with the reality that maybe it was.

SHECKY GREENE

Rebecca's husband Jacob's near heart attack frightened Peg. All she could think about was Jack's high cholesterol, his blood pressure, and the guilt she would feel if he died never knowing her terrible secret. There were so many times she had wanted to tell him, but couldn't. Why was it now, suddenly hitting her so hard? Although it was only ten in the morning, she poured a shot of Jim Beam into her coffee and went out to the backyard to try and relax.

Peter was in the kitchen, still in his pajamas, learning to make tiramisu along with Jean Claude and Beth on the TV. The chef had just spread mascarpone and whipped cream over ladyfingers, when he put down his spatula and took Beth's hand. "Beth, we've been doing this show together for some time, and now that we've become America's Culinary Couple, isn't it time to make it official?"

"What do you mean?" asked Beth.

"Yeah, what do you mean?" shouted Peter at the TV.

The chef got down on one knee. "Beth, will you marry me?" Beth was speechless. Jean Claude, still on his knee, turned to camera. "We'll be back with Beth's answer after this."

Peg poured another shot of whisky into her cup as Luke rode up the fairway on his mower. Her thoughts drifted back to the day it started.

The year was 1989. A shirtless, much younger Luke was on a riding mower, close to the Michaels' property. Peg, twenty-five years younger, wearing the swimsuit she wore at the Miss Jones Beach contest, was in her backyard talking on a corded phone.

"Another five days? Jack, you've been gone for *two weeks*."

"You think I like being stuck in Milwaukee?" said Jack. "The most exciting thing here is watching the Schlitz sign go on and off."

"But I'm lonely."

"You think I'm here for myself? This is for us, our future."

"I know how hard you work, but you're gone so much."

"Look, find something to distract yourself. Go hit some balls."

"I miss you."

"I miss you, too."

Jack was lying. He was also lying about being in

Milwaukee. He was calling from the Sands Hotel in Las Vegas.

"Jacob, I got us seats to see Sinatra," said a young, beautiful Rebecca.

"And after, Shecky Greene in the lounge," added Jack, putting his arm around her. "Is this a honeymoon, or what? Let's go play Keno."

In the backyard, young Peg poured herself a drink and then noticed Luke on the mower, looking at her. He smiled. She smiled back. Maybe it was the alcohol, maybe it was the loneliness, or a combination of both. It was the first and only time Peg had been unfaithful to Jack.

But there was more than that Peg felt guilty about. She took another sip of her coffee, then walked to the fence bordering the fairway and motioned to the greenskeeper. Luke shut off his mower and walked toward her. He was twenty-five years older now, but still as handsome as he was on that hot summer day. The fence between them, they stood there looking at each other. "I'm going to tell them," said Peg.

Inside the house, Peter, heartbroken, was still watching Cooking with Jean Claude.

"We're back," Jean Claude said. "And if you're just tuning in, I've asked Beth to marry me. Well, Sweetheart?" The studio audience applauded and shouted its approval.

"Yes," Beth said, softly.

He kissed her and the audience cheered. Peter shut off the set, took the tiramisu to his room, and smeared it on the wall.

Jack arrived home, ready to confess. Just as Dr. Salvatore predicted, the dreaded day had finally come. He found Peg in the backyard, half crocked. *Good. This will make it easier for her to take.* Then he noticed Luke, sitting on his mower on the other side of the fairway, watching them, so he asked Peg to come inside. There was something he needed to tell her. She wobbled her way out of the chaise, put her arms around him, and began sobbing.

Peg unburdened her soul and confessed the secret she had been keeping for twenty-five years. When she was finished, rather than tell her what *he* had done, Jack became indignant, calling her a filthy whore, before storming out of the house. Jack got in his car and headed straight for Bridgeport, where he planned to stay overnight, do the auction the next day, then drive back to Jersey where he'd switch cars and go home to his faithful wife, Rebecca. As for Peg, he no longer felt guilty about what he had done to her. After all, look what *she* did to him!

Peg was beside herself with grief. She had revealed to Jack the secret she'd been hiding all these years. Now he hated her for it, and probably would want a divorce. Then there was Peter. How could she have kept this from him? Finally able to gather herself, she went to

Peter's room and told him about that night with Luke, twenty-five years ago. "I loved your father too much to let it continue."

Suddenly, it hit him — the truth, which he'd been hiding all these months to protect his mother, could now actually ease her pain. "Mom, listen, there's much more to this than you know. You cheated on him once. He's been cheating on you for your entire marriage." Peg was stunned. Peter gently touched her shoulder. "He has another wife and family in New Jersey. Beth's family. She's his daughter. That's why we can't be together. Beth's my sister."

Peg was reeling. Everything she believed in was falling apart. But, despite her pain, she knew the truth was even more important now. It was her turn to ease her son's pain.

"Peter... Beth's not your sister."

Peter stared at her, in disbelief. It took awhile for him to process the significance of what he had just heard.

"Can you ever forgive me for not telling you?" she said, tears streaming down her face. Peter embraced his mother and gently kissed her on the forehead.

✶✶✶✶✶✶

Peter came through the backyard gate, onto the fairway. He glanced at the eighth hole and saw Luke watering the green, looking anxiously his way. As Peter approached Luke, he thought about all the times in his life the greenskeeper had gone out of his way to say "hello" and ask how he was doing. Now it all made sense. They stood for a few moments in silence. Then Peter said the words the greensskeeper had longed to hear for so many years. "Luke, you're my father."

"Your mother and I agreed it'd be best for everyone if we kept it secret," said Luke. "Not a day went by I didn't question that decision. I had some better job offers, but I wanted to stay close to you."

"I understand."

"Can I give you a hug… Son?"

"Sure… Dad."

Luke hugged Peter tightly, trying to make up for all the years of separation in one long squeeze.

"How 'bout we have that beer, now?" asked Luke.

"I would, but there's something I've got to do."

HAMILTON PARK

Peter was speeding down the Long Island Expressway when a New York state trooper pulled him over.

"You have a reason for going ninety-five in the carpool lane?"

"Yes I do, Officer. I just found out my girlfriend isn't my sister."

The trooper ordered him out of the car for a field sobriety test, which he passed with flying colors. Peter told the officer the whole story about his dysfunctional family and how he had to get to Beth to tell her the news. There was no guarantee she was still in love with him, but he had to try. The trooper was deeply touched and gave Peter a police escort all the way to the Midtown Tunnel.

Peter double-parked in front of Chef Jean Claude's loft, ran up the steps, and pressed every button on the directory until someone buzzed him in. He raced up the stairwell and pounded on the chef's door. Jean Claude answered, wearing a silk robe.

"I need to talk to Beth," said Peter.

"You don't even wait till the body's cold, do you?" said the chef.

"What do you mean?"

"You're here because you saw the show, n'est pas?"

"Yeah. You proposed and she accepted, right after the Sham Wow commercial."

"You obviously didn't see the whole show. We had just sprinkled paprika on the flank steak when she began to cry. She said she didn't love me. I was devastated. But it *was* great television."

"She's not here?"

"No," he said, shutting the door.

Peter raced down the stairs, just as his car was about to be towed away. A hundred dollar bribe later, he had his car back, and drove straight to his old apartment in Astoria. When he arrived, Mrs. Odetts was sitting on the stoop.

"She's not here," said the old woman.

"Do you know where she is?"

"*I* don't... but *you* do."

******

BETH WAS SITTING ON HER BENCH, in Hamilton Park, so deep in thought she didn't notice Peter until he sat down next to her.

"I can't be with you. I can't be with him. I probably

won't be able to be with anybody," she said, staring off into the distance.

"You *can* be with me," he whispered.

"Peter, stop it."

"He's not my father."

"What?!"

Peter carefully repeated everything his mother had told him. When he was done, Beth burst into tears and threw her arms around him. They finally broke apart and looked into each other's eyes. Then they kissed... a long, deep, definitely not a brother-sister kiss.

******

Jack was heading north on I-95 when the impact of not being Peter's father finally hit him. The memories of all the good times they'd had together flashed across his mind. Despite everything, he loved that boy more than life itself. And for the first time in a very, very long time, Jack started to cry. Then he realized the inevitable; Peg would tell Peter, Peter would tell Beth, and Beth would tell Rebecca. He was going to lose them all. Father McKenzie was right. This was punishment for his life of deceit, a life he could never go back to. When he reached the Bridgeport exit, instead of getting off, he just kept going.

EPILOGUE

JACK NEVER RETURNED... to either family. When Rebecca learned the truth from Beth, he was lucky he *didn't* go back. At first devastated, like all of Jack's victims, her devastation quickly turned to extreme hatred. If he had walked through the door, she would have hacked off his testicles with a meat cleaver and fed them to Lucky, the schnauzer. Oh, and Jack was right about Rabbi Feldman. As soon as Jack was out of the picture, Feldman hit on Rebecca, inviting her to fast with him on Yom Kippur. Talk about your cheap date. Peg, now guilt free, was able to give up drinking. She's currently dating Luke, much to the envy of her golfing buddies. As for Beth and Peter, they had a traditional/non-traditional, Jewish/Catholic wedding.

"By the powers vested in us," said Father McKenzie.

"We now pronounce you husband and wife," added Rabbi Feldman.

Peter stomped on the napkin-wrapped glass, and,

as everyone cheered, he kissed the new Mrs. Michaels. Beth was right, she didn't have to change her last name. The happy couple walked up the aisle, past a beaming Rebecca, Peg, Luke, Phil, Lenny, Linda Romano, Mrs. Odetts, and Todd in his wheelchair, who was on his cell phone.

"Yeah, Dad, he just stepped on the fucking glass two seconds ago."

"Just tell them I love them," said Jack. "And you."

Jack clicked off his cell phone. He was sitting at a kitchen table. A woman was at the stove.

"Who was that, Jacques?"

"Nobody, Honey."

THE END

Made in the USA
Charleston, SC
10 April 2015